shelter *Me*

A **SHELTER** NOVEL

NEW YORK TIMES BESTSELLING AUTHOR

STEPHANIE TYLER

*We are all like the bright moon,
we still have our darker sides.*

—Khalil Gibran

1

"ARE YOU ALL RIGHT?" was the first thing Brayden said in lieu of hello when I answered my cell phone.

Brayden was tall, dark and incredibly handsome, but most important, he was also the safe man in my life. He was champion, cheerleader, family, and I'd been inside his art gallery—and away from him—for all of fifteen minutes.

"You worry too much about me," I informed him as I paced the main space that was currently a mess from all my paintings dragged in from the back room.

"When was the last time you ate?"

I paused. "The last time you fed me. So I'm kind of starving."

"What else is new, Ryn?" I heard the grin in his voice. "I'll head over to the gallery with food."

"Thanks."

"You sure you're okay?"

I sighed. "I haven't read the article yet, if that's what you're asking."

"Good. Wait, and we'll read it together over greasy food and beers."

My stomach rumbled in appreciative agreement. "Love you, Bray."

"Ditto, babe."

"When you get here, you can help me pick the order for the showing."

"No way—that's all you, so get to work. Time's running out," Brayden told me cheerfully and I mentally flipped him off.

The magazine article in question taunted me from the main countertop. I ignored it in favor of concentrating on the space, visualizing how I wanted my paintings to hang. I was very familiar with the gallery set-up, but having the luxury of planning my first solo show was amazing.

I'd seen this space over the years through pictures and on Skype, and once, in person, two years ago on Christmas. Brayden had bought the Lower East Side gallery years earlier and now, with other galleries escaping to the area like refugees from the expensive Chelsea zip code, it was the perfect spot. The gallery was on the street level, neatly tucked between the numerous Manhattan apartment buildings and other storefronts. There were a couple of cute cafés and restaurants clustered along the block, some with outside tables. Lots of art, lots of action.

I'd been in New York City for a grand total of three weeks, all of which I found completely overwhelming, with a tiny bit of exhilaration thrown in.

Outside, the city moved at a breakneck pace. I tried to capture the frantic combination of the cacophony mixed with calm confidence in my art. The frenzy combined with mine, and in the weeks leading up to the show, Brayden told me I'd done some of my best work. He'd also insisted on bringing some of those brand-new pieces into the show. The retrospective was called *Shouldering the Past* and it was so very appropriate. Sitting here, surrounded by my work, I felt ragged but happy.

He'd never pushed me to have a showing, but he'd told me that I needed to have one whether I was there or not. He left me a full year to plan for it. And although I was still unsure, my new place was a six-month rental that was two blocks away from the gallery. My apartment was one floor below Brayden's, and paid for with some of the money he'd earned for me by selling my work over the years. I'd quickly gotten pretty well immersed in all of this city life. It had taken some getting used to—the noise, the general bustle of things—but my place was quiet. Surround sound and low, white noise music to block everything out was one of Brayden's first installations for me. At night, I locked myself away and painted until dawn, all while staring at a far different skyline than I was used to. But the moon was still there—I told myself that was all that mattered. It was, to me, a time of renewal. A fresh start. I painted more in September, but I also slept less, eager not to miss anything.

In the past four years, Brayden had become my best friend as well as my benefactor. He knew most of my secrets and I knew most of his. He'd brought me further in my career than I'd ever thought possible. I'd gone from a second-floor apartment in the Catskills and a job in a coffeehouse to an in-demand, up-and-coming artist. He'd used my sketchy past to create a mystique, used my nemesis—my panic attacks—to make my reputation as an artist crazier, and thereby stronger.

It amazed me how the world worked: because people thought I was unbalanced, they looked more closely at my art and I got noticed in a big way.

I wasn't unbalanced. Not in the way the articles I'd seen up until this point had made it seem, but since Brayden was the one giving the interviews for me, I could understand how it must come across. I'd done some phone ones, but I'd refused to meet for any of them in person before this last week. I'd talk about the café, because I'd say it was the beginning of my story, but in truth, I'd never let anyone visit there or my old apartment. I didn't want anyone invading the space with my art. I was private and superstitious, possibly the worst combination ever. Add to that my panic attacks and—on paper—I was a straight-up mental case.

Which was somehow acceptable because I was an artist. It was even expected.

But the magazine that currently taunted me from the countertop contained the first interview I'd given face-to-face. First *and* last, if I had my way, which was why Brayden had done all the other press for the show and was currently firming up last-minute details for tomorrow night.

My job was the grunt work, which I much preferred. Surrounded by the pieces that'd been my heart and soul over the past six months, I looked for the pattern. Over the past six years, I always looked for it, because I knew that in some way, every painting I'd completed contained a piece of my past in it, a past I had no memory of at all.

In front of me now were the landscapes I'd

been focused on, fraught with big, bold color slashed through like a bolt of lightning, ruining the perfection, marring it to the point where it made it beautiful. It was strangely hypnotic. It shouldn't work, but it did—at least according to some critics.

Simplicity meets sophistication.

A fresh new talent on the rise.

I tried not to read the bad reviews but I failed, despite the fact that they were cutting.

Amateurish.

Silly.

Unstructured.

The kind of untalented artist who's making a name for herself based on her breakdowns.

I hadn't had a breakdown, but I'd be damned if I'd answer any of them. Instead, their comments made me paint harder. They made me angry. But in reality, they were what forced me here, in person, to deal with the crap being said about me. Not that parts of it weren't true—I owned up to my panic attacks.

The ones I could remember, at least.

Shaking that off, I got back to work, which consisted of kneeling on the ground, the paintings spread in front of me, glancing between them and the empty white walls where they'd soon hang, unable to make a decision.

I felt the cold of the tiled floor through the fashionably frayed knees of the Rag & Bone jeans Brayden had given me. He'd started muttering to himself earlier when he'd seen the paint splatters and other abuses heaped on them—"I've been trying some sculpture" apparently wasn't the right explanation, but the jeans looked destroyed out of the bag anyway. I'd thrown on a tank top with skinny straps that kept falling off my shoulders, had already stripped off the denim shirt that matched my eyes and flung it into the corner and I was at least certain that there was no paint in my hair. I'd showered, let it air dry in a straight, buttery blonde sheet down my back, something apparently envied in Manhattan.

I absently tucked it into a loose braid over one shoulder while I studied the painting in front of me. I'd wanted to let Brayden pick the order, but he'd refused earlier that morning, and told me I was running out of time. At that memory, I murmured "Bastard" in his absence.

That's when a low, rough voice said, "People usually know me at least five minutes before calling me that."

Still on the floor, I whipped around to see the tall, brutally handsome man standing maybe ten feet away. How long had he been there? I hadn't heard him come in, but now that he was coming closer, I couldn't tear my eyes away.

The fight or flight response had remained intact when my memory hadn't. Everyone, every stranger wasn't necessarily a stranger. They could know me. They could be a part of my past.

Whether this man was or not, my base response to him was a purely physical one.

"The door was open," the man explained.

And it might've been. Brayden told me to lock myself in but I often forgot. Panic must have flashed across my face because he stopped advancing and held up his hands like a show of surrender. But he didn't try to tell me he was harmless, because he wasn't. Never could be. And the man who waited for him had moved too, turned his back in an effort to appear less threatening.

"My name's Lucas. I buy a lot of art from Brayden."

"Mine?" I asked.

"Not yet."

"I guess you'll have to try harder."

A smile ghosted across his chiseled face and I liked that. Wanted to see it more, wanted to be the one who could always bring a smile to his face.

These men could be here to harm me and I was too busy with my tongue hanging out to threaten them with the police.

Because you rely on your gut, Ryn, my therapist,

foster mom and Brayden always told me. *That will get you through just about any situation.*

My gut said this man knew I was Ryn Taylor, artist, but didn't know anything beyond that about me except what he'd read in interviews. Maybe he was here for my art, or maybe it was for me. But how could I feel so connected to someone I'd just met?

Lucas.

I rolled the name around in my mind as my eyes took in the black leather motorcycle jacket and the tighter black T-shirt underneath...the worn-in jeans and the heavy black motorcycle boots. I saw the hint of an expensive watch peek out on his wrist as he came closer.

I knew too, if I pushed up those sleeves, I'd find some ink. Incongruous, and ultimately intriguing.

The angles of his face begged to be drawn, to be touched, and I held my hands down rigidly at my sides so I wouldn't do just that. "My show's not until tomorrow night," I managed.

"I know."

"Are you here to..." I looked around for Brayden, like he would magically appear and caught another glance of the other man by the door. "Are you here for Brayden?"

"For Brayden? No." His mouth quirked up to the side a little and he ran a hand through his dark blond hair. It was long enough to curl a bit at the nape of his neck, and it was rumpled, like maybe he'd just rolled out of bed…and maybe he hadn't been alone.

"You're not his type."

His blue eyes pierced me. They were a dark blue and they missed nothing. "Whose type am I?"

Mine, I nearly blurted out. I was nervous, my stomach fluttering but not in that panicked way I recognized. Just the opposite, actually. Heat flooded me as he stared at me in my tank top and jeans with utmost appreciation, the frank gaze of someone who understood beauty and acted on it.

I wanted him to act, but at the same time, I needed him to stay away. I was too drawn to him, an electromagnetic pull that spun the earth on its axis differently. Something told me that I'd never get this man out of my life. I'd never be done with him, or him of me, and holy hell, that was a heady enough thought to make me dizzy.

I remained on my knees, stock still, looking up at him. I had the odd feeling that if I moved, even a little, I'd fall, trip, completely ruin the moment.

He gave me a heated look, and dammit, he knew what I was thinking.

Every woman who came into contact with him probably had that reaction. And that made me unnaturally, irrationally jealous because, in my mind, I'd already claimed him.

Finally, his gaze shifted to the paintings I'd been appraising. He focused on one that was part of a series that'd already sold well, thanks to Brayden. I'd wanted to call the series *Man in Trees* (and still did so) but Brayden told me it was creepy and insisted on simply, *Catskills* as the official series title. And while I could see what he meant, the person these were based on had never, ever scared me. But I couldn't tell Brayden these were based on someone real, because he'd freak out.

Even though I was building an entire series around him, I'd never seen the man's face. Still, I'd always sworn I'd be able to sense him the way I'd sensed him out there before I'd caught sight of the shadowed figure, and even though I hadn't been able to see his face clearly, I knew he was big, broad and utterly male. I'd wanted to walk across the lawn, strip him and paint him…and then climb him after I stripped myself.

When I'd shown Brayden the first picture, he'd insisted on bringing it to the gallery. I hadn't wanted that, but I'd felt foolish telling Brayden about why the painting was so special to me, why I wanted to keep it. He told me that if I was sentimental about my work, I'd never get anywhere. In the end, after a terrible fight, I agreed to let him show it in his gallery, but I'd have final say if it was to be sold.

It was stolen a week later.

I stared up at Lucas as he stared at my painting—the fourth in a collection of nine, not counting the missing first one, all attempts to recreate those initial feelings that had propelled me to paint the first one. His expression unshuttered for a brief moment, like he was letting me in, drawing me closer to the fire.

I couldn't afford to play with fire, but he was like the ghost of the man I thought I'd conjured up on that warm summer's night in the Catskills. I was seventeen, dizzy and half high from creating. I'd glanced over and watched him. He was half hidden among the trees and if I hadn't been coming off a painting, I would've been terrified. Instead, I noticed how handsome he was, chiseled and mysterious.

I dreamed about him that whole week, less as the years went by, but always when I needed comfort, or when I was coming out of the burn of my art.

He'd been there. He was now here. Could I have wanted him so badly that my dream turned into reality? A ridiculous thought and one I chided myself for.

Creation didn't work that way.

I tried to draw in a shaky breath when this

ridiculously beautiful, rough man moved a few steps in my direction, even though he was still focused on the painting.

The walls were closing in on me until he said, "Your work is beautiful," and turned from me to the paintings.

What little space he'd given me let me breathe. Even though I swore his gaze heated me, the fact that he was pointing to various paintings soothed me.

"My first show is tomorrow," was all I could think of to say, even though it was probably obvious.

"Your work is ready."

Your *work*. Like he knew *I* wasn't. "I don't think I'll ever be."

He turned back to me then. "That's not a bad thing. Protect whatever the hell makes these."

What made those was a part of the nightmare of my blacked-out past. What if discovering what was behind it stole the art from me, left me limp, with nothing? What if I had to trade nightmares and the thing I loved for peace? That haunted me, so I'd chosen not to have peace.

I remained on the ground, drawn to him, wanting to rise but refusing to do so. Sheer stubbornness and self-preservation mixed together.

He reached a hand down to help me up but I couldn't touch him. Not yet.

I pushed myself up. He was at least six foot four to my five feet four inches. The difference was dramatic.

He was so still, a predator, watching me with keen interest. I'd never been as intensely aware of a man in my life. I could smell his skin, wanted to taste it, put my mouth on his and forget everything else, including basic human decency.

I blamed the art. The heat. My lack of proper nutrition.

I stuck out my hand without saying anything, almost a dare. He took it in his and my pulse beat a tattoo. I felt the slow burn and then the aftershock quake through my whole body.

There was a definite sense of street in him, a primal, easily willing and able to fight for his life street sense.

His eyes were haunted, like maybe he already had.

There was no doubt he'd won.

"What the fuck is going on here?"

I was relieved when Brayden's entrance broke the intensity in the room. I stepped backward, away from Lucas's flame in an attempt to break the connection.

It didn't waver. It was too late for me. No saving me now. The "drowning ship, abandon hope all ye who enter here" must've shown in my eyes, because Brayden attempted to help me. It was too late. The ship was sinking, and Brayden needed to save himself.

"We're closed," Brayden said angrily to Lucas.

"The door was open."

"I'm betting it wasn't."

He and Brayden squared off, so I said, "I might've left it open," hoping to stave off a fight. Because Brayden could fight, and when he was younger he had, well and often.

Lucas acknowledged my words with a nod, but he didn't take his eyes off Brayden.

"And you're Lucas…"

"Lucas Caine," Brayden growled in answer to me before Lucas could chime in. Brayden was hovering, protective, and it was chest to chest alpha males, and both of them nearly equal in height. Dark and light, facing off. It was only then I noticed Brayden's attention moved to the other man by the door.

"He's with me," Lucas said, his voice a rough growl that smoothed my ruffled feathers. Nothing about him was particularly cultured and yet he reeked of money. Everything about him screamed feral, but the wildness didn't take anything from him. He was a complete study in contradictions.

There were tattoos under all that clothing—I was sure of it.

"And neither of you have told me why you're here," Brayden said.

"It's definitely not to see you," Lucas shot back. His voice was the kind that would deepen to a rough growl when he was angry or aroused, as if there was a force of law command behind his dirty, wild voice.

I wondered how his voice would sound during dirty, wild sex.

I wished I painted nudes. I had to start a collection—that would be my next series.

"What are you doing here?" Brayden repeated impatiently.

"I came for the show," Lucas said innocently.

"The show's not until tomorrow night."

Lucas's shrug was meant for Brayden, but his words, his gaze, were all for me. "I wanted to preview Ryn's work."

"We don't offer previews," Brayden said through clenched teeth.

"I don't let that stop me," Lucas countered.

Nothing would and God, I liked that.

Lucas glanced at me. "You haven't been in

town long."

"And she's probably not staying," Brayden added, his protective nature ringing through loud and clear.

"Is that right?" Lucas's gaze flicked across my face, seeking out the truth. "In that case, I'll definitely be back tomorrow."

With a nod in Brayden's direction, he was gone.

I was trying not to stare too long at Lucas's retreating back when Brayden asked, "Did he scare you?"

"No," I scoffed, even though Brayden would know better. "What's his deal?"

Brayden snorted. "He's an asshole."

"I got that part loud and clear." I tried to sound casual, but Brayden read me like a book.

"Don't," he warned. "You know better."

Maybe I did, maybe I didn't but… "I'm just asking what he's like."

Brayden shook his head. "He's complicated. And he's known to go through women fast. No strings, no commitments."

That figured. Wanting something bad for me was typical—exciting and dangerous, which was always my first inclination.

"He doesn't stop until he gets what he wants," Brayden continued his warning. "And when he gets it…"

"He doesn't want it anymore," I finished.

"Exactly—he wants nothing to do with them. They chase him and it's humiliating. And you deserve better."

So Lucas was a self-destructive, one-night stand, "stop anything before it has a chance of working" kind of guy.

I knew the type.

I *was* the type, which made Lucas a challenge.

"Maybe I only want one night—no strings," I said. Brayden frowned doubtfully but didn't say anything else. And that's one of the many reasons I loved him. He didn't pretend he knew every single thing about me. Rather, he let me live my life, and explore new things. And he'd be there to pick up the pieces, without saying the dreaded, *I told you so.* "It doesn't matter—he's probably just an asshole," I said softly, with no real bite behind the words, because I didn't believe it.

"Definitely an asshole," Brayden echoed in a far more strident tone.

"Is he your age?"

"Make me sound ancient," he muttered around his beer.

"You mean thirty isn't?" I teased.

He frowned. "Yes, your new obsession is my age."

"Thank you. Was that so hard?"

"Very."

This was no chance encounter, not on Lucas's part anyway. But why not wait for the show? What necessitated the private meeting? "He acted like he came here just to see me. How did he know I'd be here?"

"How does Lucas Caine know anything?"

"Does he come here a lot?"

"A couple of times a year," he said. "But he's never brought that bodyguard guy."

"Not that you've seen."

A small frown settled on his lips. "We've got work to do. And I have to get a better lock."

I wanted to tell Brayden that it wouldn't matter, and I didn't know how I knew that. I just did. I was up against someone formidable with an intensity that mirrored my own. Instead, I simply told him, "I'm starving."

As we settled on the floor, surrounded by my paintings, I dove into my burger and fries. Even as Brayden asked questions about the order of the paintings, trying to get my mind into the game, it was obvious it was somewhere else.

"Maybe I can ask Lucas to come back and help you hang the paintings," Brayden suggested at one point.

"He'd be more helpful than you're being."

Brayden rolled his eyes. "He's just a guy."

"I know that. Stop worrying—I'm not going to go home and call him or anything."

"It's not like he gave you his number," Brayden pointed out.

"You're such a prick." I threw a fry at him and he snorted. "Okay, let's take my mind off Lucas by depressing me with the magazine article."

"Such an optimist." Brayden grabbed the magazine and flipped through until he found the article. "Want me to read it out loud?"

It seemed like months ago when I spoke to Ann Maslow, the features editor of the art magazine. My carefully crafted responses which were subtly designed to hide the truth of my background but still tantalize with the intrigue. "Go for it."

I'm looking at pictures that show the artist curled on the floor of the gallery amidst the chaos, and if anything, Cathryn "Ryn" Taylor looks at home, more than one might expect from someone who, by all accounts, is socially phobic, prone to panic attacks and notoriously private. A woman who

would not meet me face to face for our interview,
choosing to remain on the other end of the phone
line and give only partial answers.

"So what—she's accusing me of faking that?" I
interrupted.

Brayden had the nerve to look amused. "And
she'll also be at the opening."

"Thanks for the warning, I guess," I muttered.
"I don't know if I can do this. I'm not the sweet,
quiet artist everyone expects."

"They don't expect that. They're looking for
the half-crazed woman who's one step away from
her nineteenth nervous breakdown."

"That's great. Very comforting, Bray. Points for
the Stones reference."

"Hey, I've seen you defend yourself. You've got
a hell of a temper."

"And you're about to find yourself on the
receiving end of it," I warned.

It was Brayden's turn to give me the finger.

None of the people who'd interviewed me
knew about what I'd gone through in my past. Not
that I did—the amnesia took care of my memories
with a startling efficiency, leaving me a blank slate
from the age of seventeen, after I'd woken up in a
hospital after being unconscious for several days.
I'd been left outside the emergency room, saved,

and later taken in by a woman who would end up introducing me to my best friend in the world.

Brayden knowing all about it was a huge step for me—and the biggest help of all. I pushed the magazine article aside in disgust. "She made me seem completely unstable."

"Flaky," he corrected, "Quirky."

"You mean fucked up."

"If you weren't, they'd be disappointed. People don't expect artists to be normal, and if you were, your art wouldn't be seen. Any springboard you can use, hon. It's about getting noticed. Then, it's up to your talent if you sink or swim."

It was amazing that my anxiety would be what got me noticed in the first place. Every story written about me noted my panic disorder. Of course, I couldn't share where the roots of that disorder lay. Could only hope that my past was far behind me, that no one from that time would recognize me. I looked different.

As for everything else? I had no clue what I'd been like before the amnesia. I was trapped in present day, and my art reflected that—the dark place I couldn't escape, no matter how hard I tried. Like a mouse trapped in a never-ending maze with no incentive to get out.

Except for Lucas Caine. Was he finally the jolt I needed?

2

SEVERAL HOURS LATER, BRAYDEN was leaving me off at my apartment door after he'd ultimately helped me put an order to my paintings and calmed me down.

"Just make sure you don't neglect your muse. I know how cranky you get when you don't paint," he warned as I let myself inside.

His concern had nothing to do with money—he was absolutely right that missing even a day of painting left me anxious and irritable. Two days was a lifetime. At times, I avoided painting because the subject matter was difficult and exhausting, and it was Brayden who'd finally told me that I was a bitch when I avoided the canvas.

"And lock the damned door," he called through it. Granted, I'd been about to walk away from it without doing so, and I managed to click the double bolts before I kicked off my sneakers and wandered toward the easel.

When I blinked, it seemed like maybe five minutes had passed, but I knew better. At times, I could lose five, six, seven hours to the muse I'd come to nickname "the beast."

Feed the beast before it eats you alive.

Now, I realized night surrounded me. I'd been painting nearly in the dark. At some point during the frenzy, I'd turned on the small studio light, but the rest of the apartment was in total darkness. The heat was more oppressive here than it was upstate, with no nighttime relief. I'd bought myself a selection of flowers that I separated and spread around the apartment in bunches. I smelled the flowers strongly, probably because I'd kept the windows closed and the air off.

I jerked the windows open for relief from the sweet smell and continued painting. At some point, I went to the kitchen for something to drink and squished the stems between my toes.

The flowers were on the ground, as if someone had dumped them from their vases, except there were no empty vases.

Daffodils. I hadn't *bought* daffodils. I'd grabbed Gerbera daisies…and those were still in their jars. But the daffodils were spread along the floor like a path that led to nowhere.

I stared stupidly. Maybe I'd taken my anti-anxiety meds without realizing it? I rubbed my arms at the sudden chill that went through my body, and I rechecked the door. I flicked on all the lights in the apartment, but it was just me, my paintings and the flowers.

I rubbed my eyes as exhaustion and panic began to overtake me. I grabbed for some of the homeopathic remedies I'd been using instead and sent a text to my therapist about a Skype session.

I'd probably knocked the flowers over in my rush to get to painting. It wasn't like I hadn't spilled or forgotten things before when painting was on my mind. But still, a chat with my therapist wouldn't do me any harm.

I'd gotten to a good place with my anxiety, but the months before arriving in New York had me refilling prescriptions for anti-anxiety meds and speaking with Dr. B a little more often. He was the same therapist I'd used in the Catskills, because the idea of switching to a new one made me too anxious. I needed an anchor to the past, a tether to the only place I remembered as home. And Dr. B was a family man. Former military. Kind and trustworthy. But certainly, no pushover.

And I pushed.

These days, I was proud of myself. Beyond my first week, I'd been able to manage my anxiety without meds and I felt calmer and safer now. The interview and the upcoming show was a lot to manage, but painting helped me.

But seeing the flowers was stirring something—a memory or a dream…and I was getting the uncomfortable, chest-tightening sensation. My skin was clammy and I heard the harshness of my breath in my own ears.

Does someone know? Did they recognize me?

Daffodils. An innocuous flower. Why was I having such a reaction to them?

Because you're tired. Shaken up. Even with the modicum of success I'd just gained, I realized how difficult being successful actually was. Being on top of the mountain, or close to it, was more pressure than wanting it.

I stopped myself. Reminded myself of Dr. B's words, that "fear, stress and no sleep do strange things to people's minds."

I had plenty of fear, stress and no sleep—I'd been riding on pure adrenaline for days. I assured myself that I'd probably knocked the flowers over at some point in my painting frenzy, and that Brayden had been the one to send them. He was always making sure the apartment was well stocked with food and flowers—*the finer things*, he called them. He knew if left to my own devices I'd live on takeout and never have anything living in my apartment except mold growing on old food in the fridge. That was easily evidenced several hours later, after a great, calming session with Dr. B, a hot shower and Brayden in my kitchen making breakfast.

"You're such a guy," Brayden was complaining after pouring an entire expired milk into the sink. "Good thing you've got me."

"We live a door away from a deli."

"Exactly." He tossed the empty milk and unpacked two new ones. He started the coffeemaker and soon the smell of brew filled the room.

I didn't bother asking him about the flowers. I told myself I'd just forgotten to do so, but really, I didn't want to deal with any of it today.

Tomorrow. I'd deal with all of it tomorrow.

By five that evening, I was dressed in a stylish little black dress, my hair up in a loose, elegant knot, sparse makeup—enough to emphasize those baby blues, the makeup artist had insisted—and inside the gallery as the doors opened. Brayden told me I was stunning, and for once, I believed him.

There was something magical about this night,

the magic of all possibilities unfolding at my feet. Of course, this was because the doors were still closed.

When they did open, I was worried the panic would slowly wrap around me, fighting to squeeze me in an anaconda grip. That was how I'd made Brayden understand what the attacks were like when we watched the movie of the same name. He'd laughed with me, then sobered and said, "That sucks."

I knew then we'd be best friends.

Now, he either kept a hand on one of my shoulders or threaded a hand in mine as small talk ensued. He was part promoter, all bodyguard, stopping people from getting too close, smoothly edging me away when it looked like I was about to get surrounded.

He'd told me I could escape to the quiet of the back room, and I'd had to take advantage of it only once so far. Admittedly, I was disappointed, as I'd hoped to find Lucas back there, smirking at getting past the security measures of the storeroom areas.

But Lucas came through the front door tonight, two hours into the show, when it was at its most crowded, and I swear, the entire gallery stilled for a long moment when he walked in. I know I did.

The whole gallery seemed to come to an immediate stop, like a breath drawn inward and not exhaled unless given permission.

When Lucas finally gave it with a nod to my corner of the gallery, business and pleasure restarted as normal, although there was still that hit of electricity spiking the air.

Lucas seemed used to it. Maybe he even expected it. But it didn't deter him from his path, which was coming directly to me, his eyes locked and loaded on mine. I was unable to look away and he was devouring me. That was something I'd normally be embarrassed to even think, but there was no substitute for the word.

His physical presence had the most extreme push to it. I'd never registered anything like that from anyone. He was so still, a predator, watching me with keen interest. I'd never been as intensely aware of a man in my life. I could smell his skin, wanted to taste it, put my mouth on his and forget everything else, including basic human decency.

I blamed the art. The heat. My lack of proper nutrition.

When he was directly in front of me, he smiled. "It looks like your dreams are coming true."

Such double meaning to those words. He hadn't said congratulations. Because he knew I saw this as a mixed blessing. Was it understanding or mocking? Did he know how scared of those dreams I was?

"Thanks for coming," I told him as Brayden said, "More people to see," with a glare in Lucas's direction.

Lucas's expression registered amusement, and reluctantly, I pulled my focus from him back to Brayden, who was literally tugging me in the direction of willing buyers and giving me murmured updates about how many paintings sold. I'd noticed that the painting Lucas had liked was already tagged.

"Who bought that?" I asked Bray, and he frowned. Checked his list.

"Phone sale," he said slowly. "Says the buyer will pick up tomorrow. Grant Loughlin."

Grant. *Not* Lucas.

"There's Ann Maslow," Brayden noted as he steered me clear, as we'd discussed. I'd planned on avoiding her like the plague. She was pretty—tall, with dark hair and serious-looking glasses that I bet had non-prescription lenses.

I didn't know how much longer I could do this. A lot of people here were happy for me. Some weren't, and I felt their thinly veiled intentions as surely as if they'd stabbed me with them.

Head up, Ryn. You earned this. You deserve it.

Because after what hell I'd most likely survived, to give a critic, or a jealous competitor, that much power, seemed too foolish. But still, this mingling wasn't my domain, my forte. I'd given them my art, and now I wanted to revoke their access to *me.*

I took a long drink of water and popped a peppermint into my mouth, contemplating my exit strategy. If anyone noticed I'd disappeared, it would only look better in their articles.

And then I was making small talk, *participating in my own success,* as Brayden insisted, when someone tapped me on the shoulder. I fully expected it to be Ann, but it wasn't. It was an auburn-haired, alabaster-skinned woman, maybe a few years older than me. She looked like she belonged in a painting herself, managing to be vulnerable and haughty at once.

"You're the artist?" She looked me up and down in a most obvious way that made me happy I didn't remember ever going to high school.

I smiled tightly. "Yes. Ryn Taylor."

"Ah." She crossed one arm across her chest— the other lifted the champagne flute to her mouth. "First show, right? Must be nice to have a bestie who owns a gallery."

Out of the corner of my eye, I caught a glimpse of Ann Maslow deep in conversation with Lucas. "It doesn't hurt," I said honestly. "But he's not the one buying all the paintings."

"No, Lucas is," Brayden muttered behind me

when the woman rolled her eyes and walked away.

"He's buying me. Trying to, anyway," I said and Brayden didn't deny it.

"Does it matter? Because he's only getting the paintings, Ryn. He can't take what's not freely given."

That didn't mean Lucas Caine wouldn't try. I stared into the crowded gallery space. This was everything I'd dreamed about over the past eight years and figured I could never do. With the help of the doctor, conditioning exercises and rescue medication in case of an actual panic attack—and my best friend in the world—I was doing it.

"Hello, Miss Taylor."

I turned to find Ann Maslow standing there, staring at me with a hard look. "Please, it's Ryn. Thanks for coming."

She raised her glass and motioned around. "Couldn't miss it—I'd been hoping to get an early viewing for the article but..." She trailed off and shrugged. "Your work here is definitely... different."

Out of the corner of my eye, I caught a glimpse of the auburn-haired woman talking to Lucas, looking between him and me, with a possessive hand on his arm.

Great.

I excused myself from Ann and her insulting

comment that had been delivered with a smile. She was vacillating between ignoring me and staring at me, like she was writing a second, more unflattering article in her mind anyway, and I knew spending more time with her wasn't in my best interest, on any level.

I pushed into the back room, went toward the rear door where it was more private and out of the way of the bathroom traffic.

Within moments, I wasn't alone. I don't know how, as I'd locked the door behind me and there wasn't a window big enough for him to fit through that wasn't barred. But Lucas was here and he smelled gorgeous, like fresh air and sunshine, despite the rain. I couldn't help but feel a wash of satisfaction rush over me because he'd come after me, leaving Miss Alabaster behind.

That wasn't the only reason I'd come into the back room, but I couldn't deny that, somewhere in the recesses of my mind, I'd been hoping he would.

As I looked at him, a slow burn charged the atmosphere and I knew I was in real trouble.

I'd had experiences, had my heart broken by a man I'd admitted everything to. He was another creative type—an author, and I thought he got me. That was until he told me that my emotions would drain his creativity. That happened after a weekend together that I thought went really well. But I got over him and in the meantime he'd hit some bestseller lists and had some pretty good success with his books. It was my turn now, and I had no problem taking it.

This man... I wasn't sure I could handle him. But I wanted to try. I was more than willing to try. There was a barely concealed wildness inside him, just riding the surface, pulling me to him.

His eyes raked over me. It took everything not to look down and check that I was actually wearing clothes. He was the Big Bad Wolf and I didn't know my way through the woods.

It'd been too long for me—that was all, I reasoned, knowing full well I was lying to myself. Brayden had shown me a few of the college bars around the Catskills area, but none of those guys did much for me. They were fun, easy to walk away from.

Then again, I wasn't looking for anyone hard to walk away from. Lucas was outwardly calm but predatory. I was being hunted—I had no doubt about that. His walk was more like stalking in nature. He could take on anyone—anything— and there wasn't a man or woman in the gallery tonight who didn't sense it.

"What are you doing back here?" I asked in an attempt to hide all my feelings.

"Want me to leave?" he asked, even as his long legs ate the distance between us. Even if there'd been an unlimited supply of oxygen in the room, I still wouldn't have been able to breathe. And when I didn't—couldn't—answer, he continued, "Are you having fun yet?"

"No."

"I can change that," Lucas said roughly before his weight shifted onto me, pressing me against the wall. His sleeve had been pushed up, exposing a heavy, expensive-looking watch and a sleeve of tattoos that began below his wrist. I touched the ink, expecting to feel something akin to an electric shock.

I wasn't disappointed, not by that or by Lucas's next words.

"Jesus Christ. I'm in so much trouble." He muttered it angrily, almost more to himself than to me.

"I didn't ask you to come here."

"Want me to leave, Ryn?" His thumb brushed my nipple through the thin fabric of my dress, and I moaned softly. To have his hands on me, the way they'd roamed my body in my dreams last night. This was so much better than I'd imagined.

Not having a memory gave me excuses to be a bit of a wild thing. To indulge in all my impulses. To go out and sleep around (when my art let me

out of its vise-like grip). *I don't know who I am…
I'm allowed to lose control…they're lucky I'm as
normal as I am.*

Of course, I'm not sure who the ever-present
'they' was. Society? Susan? Whoever threw me
away?

Brayden understood my impulsiveness. His
matched mine in its ferocity, but he didn't have a
vicious master to rein him in. He had to do it all
by himself and I was in awe of his self-control. I
seemed to lack any, and conversely, I didn't want
any.

All of that lack of control flooded me now. I
wanted to go back to my days of no responsibility,
and so I did. But that couldn't compete with my
raging hormones, the wet between my legs, the
anger at Ann Maslow and the whole roomful of
fucking critics who were trying to fuck with the
thing that gave me the most pleasure in life. I
was, in that moment, a petulant child, rebellious
teen, presumptuous ego-laden artist, and first and
foremost a woman who wanted a man.

Nothing in life was simpler than that. Maybe
that's why it always felt so right…at least until
things went so very wrong.

"Christ, turn your brain off," he muttered
roughly.

"Distract me."

He cursed, then ran his thumbs over my nipples before rolling them between his fingers. I arched into his touch, wanting more immediately.

He gave it. He kissed me. Really kissed me. I exhaled a soft moan in his mouth and grabbed for his shoulders. He was so big and broad, his body hot, pressing mine. His mouth took mine hungrily. I made no move to stop him. I let myself feel helpless, pinned, out of control, because if this was going to be my own experience with Lucas, I was going to make sure I enjoyed every second of it.

Forget zero to sixty—this was over a hundred MPH downhill, an out of control roller coaster I didn't want to stop.

His palm slid up my dress, cupped my sex around my underwear. I swallowed hard as his fingers brushed the thin slip of fabric covering my wet sex...and then I whimpered.

"Christ, I want to take you out of here and get you into a bed. I want to take my time. But you can't leave and I can't wait. And I can always wait." He was definitely frustrated by that. A man like him, so used to control and I was making him lose it. "You're so goddamned bad for me."

"My first show ever and I'm in the back room with your hand up my dress, so ditto."

He kissed me again, the heel of his palm

pressing me. I ground against it in the tight space, against the walls between what might one day be priceless paintings. I heard the sounds of the party beyond the door, which meant they could hear us.

Thankfully, my groans were muffled in his mouth, swallowed by him as he encouraged more. Like he couldn't get enough.

When his fingers slid inside to stroke my bare sex, I lost it. One touch of my clit and I shattered against him.

When I blinked and surfaced, he was still touching me. And I was greedy. I wanted more.

I heard the door open and I froze. Lucas remained relaxed. His body totally covered mine, but what was happening was unmistakable.

We were quiet and I don't think whoever it was saw us at first. The bathroom door closed and Lucas shook his head. If we moved now, it would definitely be obvious. And then she walked out. Stopped. Turned and stared. And then she laughed, an *I can't believe this shit* kind of laugh. And then she left.

"I have to get back out there."

He stroked my cheek. "Fine. But this? This isn't over."

My cheeks burned. I locked myself in the bathroom in a futile attempt to make it look like I hadn't just had an orgasm.

Even if I didn't look it, I didn't doubt that the woman who saw us told as many people as she could. She'd definitely told Bray, because he took me by the shoulder, handed me a glass of champagne and said, "Worst possible choice of man at the worst possible time."

"I can't believe she told you."

"She didn't, directly. But I saw her face when she came out of the back room. And I saw yours. And then I saw him."

"Sorry," I said in a voice that was distinctly un-sorry.

"Important night," he hissed. "You are not a gay man."

"Then I need to find other role models besides you," I snapped back.

"Mingle. Not with Lucas," he ordered.

And I tried, I really did…but then I started hearing…

"She's fucking Lucas Caine."

"She's fucking every major art critic."

"Panic attacks are a lie."

The words swirled around me as the invisible noose around my head and neck. I'd be paralyzed soon, unable to breathe.

I had pills in my pocket, small, easy to swallow, but I hated the way they made me feel.

I was ruining Brayden's night—and I cared

about that more than I cared about myself. I figured he could smooth things over, and no doubt find a way to make all of this into a positive, so I went into the back room and slid outside the heavy door into the back alley. I planned to walk home in the light rain, but I was surprised by the auburn-haired woman who'd followed me outside.

I planned to keep walking but she blocked me with her body.

Threat. It was all my mind registered. It flashed white hot in front of my eyes.

Fight.

Get away.

Pure instinct raced through me but I forced myself to stand still. "Get out of my way."

"My name's Meghan. And you need to get away from Lucas Caine."

"Move." I tried to push past her, but she shoved me by the shoulder, catching me off guard. She was taller than me, and it didn't help that I'd kicked off my heels already while she still wore her spiked ones.

Her eyes flashed. "Leave Lucas Caine alone."

"He doesn't need a bodyguard."

She leaned in. "He's got one. He doesn't need some shut-in posing as an artist to come in and use him."

"Use him?" I couldn't help it—I laughed. If

anything, the most honest assessment of the night was that we'd used each other. And he certainly hadn't seemed upset.

"Your interviews make you sound like you're some kind of feral Nell," she hissed fiercely, her voice low. "No one rises up out of nowhere. I'm not going to stop digging until I find out what you're hiding." And if that wasn't enough, she also reached out, pinning me to the brick wall behind me, scratching the bare skin on my shoulder. "I will end you, Ryn. That's not an idle threat."

Someone already tried, and I was still here. I'd be damned if I let myself ever be a victim again.

I swung, the side of my closed fist connecting with her temple, stunning her momentarily. She let go of me and I took my advantage, grabbing her by the throat. My emotions had been too close to the surface over the past weeks anyway and I'd reached critical mass. I don't remember much after that but the burning anger that overtook me. I heard gasps, talking, but I was in a vacuum where nothing else existed, my mind full of my own demons.

This time, they came with the flash of a brief memory, of me fighting and clawing and screaming even as I heard murmurs in the background.

"Unstable bitch."

"Crazy."

"I'm definitely buying a painting now."

"Front page news."

…and then I was being held in strong arms I didn't bother fighting, with Lucas's voice in my ear. "People are watching—more reporters are coming—let's go." And just like that, the threat was diffused. My heart still pounded, adrenaline racing through me, soon to retreat and leave me weak and shaky.

I heard him talking to someone else and then I was in a car with him and we were speeding away before I'd fully surfaced.

3

I HATED LEAVING BRAYDEN to deal with this situation but my behavior and Lucas's hold didn't leave me much choice. Besides, having me stay would definitely make things worse. I didn't want to know what the fallout would be right now. Twenty-four hours at a time—that was all I could handle on a good day. Otherwise, it was the moment in front of me, and that included Lucas speeding along the city streets.

A light rain had started to fall. I heard the wipers swish, the patter against the expensive sports car I was in, but beyond that, there was only silence. Before the recriminations in my brain could begin, we pulled into a private garage attached to a brownstone. Lucas turned off the car and came around to my side and began to gather me, despite my protests. He carried me inside and put me down on a couch inside a calm, masculine-looking room. I sank into the buttery leather and he put a blanket over me and poured me a good stiff drink.

"Did I ruin everything?" I asked after a few moments, and a few sips of the whiskey.

His answer was indirect. "She came at you first, Ryn." He stared at me, swirling the liquid in his glass as he stood by the window.

"I saw her talking to you." I followed his lead, refusing to use Meghan's name out loud.

"I talked to a lot of people tonight." He was evading. I let it pass because I didn't really care—I was here with him and Meghan wasn't. "Where'd you learn to fight like that?"

"Like what?"

"Like a street kid."

I shrugged, took another sip and rolled it around before letting the burn slide down my throat.

A street kid.

This wasn't the first time I'd fought. Meghan had gotten off easy. There was a time when I'd been walking home from a shift at the coffeehouse, in broad daylight on a sunny Saturday afternoon. A couple of college guys who'd no doubt been drinking all day, based on the way they walked, talked and smelled, approached me. My gut had tightened.

"We only want a kiss, baby," one of them had said as they surrounded me. They'd gotten a lot more. I'd left them bloodied and dazed on the ground and I'd gone home and iced my hands as I tried to recreate the moves I'd used on them.

I'd also been brandishing a weapon and thankfully, Brayden talked me out of carrying that same knife tonight, because I typically kept it on me at all times. If I'd pulled that out in front of Ann Maslow…

I didn't even want to think about that.

I'd never used it. It had become, over the years, my crutch. My link to the past. It had been found by my body, unused. No fingerprints. It was the single link to my past that wasn't a physical part of me.

But I didn't tell Lucas any of that, and he didn't push. Instead, I reached for my bag. "I should call Brayden."

"He knows you came with me," Lucas said, but he did walk out of the room to give me some privacy anyway.

Brayden answered on the fifth ring. It sounded noisy in the background when he said, "Show's still going on, babe."

"Seriously?"

"Yeah, seriously."

"I can't believe it."

"I told you, scandal's a good thing. There's no putting Ryn back in the box now."

I rubbed my neck, which ached with tension. "I went home with Lucas."

"I know—he called me." Brayden sounded almost angry at that, but when he spoke again, his voice was gentler. "Are you okay?"

I gave myself a quick once-over. My head hurt, my pride was wounded but otherwise… "Getting there."

"I can pick you up when I'm done here, or send a car now," he offered.

"I'm okay."

"Just be careful," he said.

I'd already failed at that in so many ways tonight and it was a pattern he knew I planned on continuing. "Thanks, Bray."

"You deserve every minute of this success. Fuck anyone who says differently."

I slid the phone back into my bag, shaking my head at the turn of events.

"Is he coming to rescue you?" Lucas asked, a laugh in his voice as he came back into the room.

"He offered."

"I'm sure he did." As he passed by the couch, he downed his drink but didn't pour another. Instead, he went back to his spot by the window, like he was purposely staying just far enough away from me.

I wanted to move closer.

He was a challenge and danger rolled into one, an explosive combination with the potential to break all my self-imposed rules, tear my heart to pieces and leave me wrung out but satiated.

Really, was there any other way when it came to matters of the heart? Because if I didn't feel that initial, heart-pounding passion, it wasn't worth it. If I didn't think that it would be a chase, I'd walk away, because I'd learned the hard way that the chase was better than the catch. Jared (my ex) had taught me that painful lesson and I blamed my naiveté on my age, my lost memories, being nostalgic after him being my first.

Technically, he might not have been, but based on my memories, he'd been the one.

Since then, I tended to look for men with serious swagger to match the swagger I'd been told I had, because it became a battle of wills... and I was always able to walk away first. Always.

Lucas Caine would be no different. Couldn't be. There was no way to build a future without the knowledge of my past—no way I wouldn't bring danger along with me.

No way I wanted my heart broken. My art did that often enough for me. But I did want to sleep with him and I would, to prove that I could do so and walk away. Ever since the man who'd broken my trust more than my heart (to be honest though, at the time, I'd been devastated on both counts, being young, foolish and naive), I'd been able to prove that I could do this. Now, even though every fiber of my being screamed that Lucas Caine was different, a hurricane I couldn't escape, a danger that would embrace me like a warm blanket… still, I insisted I was up for the challenge.

"I shouldn't really stay," I told him as I moved from the couch to stand directly in front of him.

"You definitely should, Ryn." He slid a finger along my jawline. "I'm in way more fucking trouble than you."

Trouble, again. "You bought paintings." A stab in the dark but…

"Yes."

"Because…?"

"Because your work speaks to me. I don't have to pay people to fuck me."

That was definitely the truth, although there were a lot of men who preferred the ease of paying for it. "This is ridiculous."

He frowned. "Which part?"

"Coming here with you. What I did with you in the back room. All of it." I put my fists to my temples and then I did the unthinkable…

something I hadn't done in days.

I laughed. It was a crazy belly laugh, the kind that fed on itself and I didn't stop until I could barely catch my breath.

When I did, Lucas was staring at me intently, a small smile playing on his lips.

I wiped my eyes, imagining that the perfect smoky eye that had been so carefully applied was now rolling down my cheeks. "Sorry. It's all just so absurd. I mean, I'm worried about what people will think of me and my art, so I sabotage myself by sleeping with you and getting into a fistfight during my first show."

"What we did in that back room had nothing to do with sabotage, babe," he said huskily. "You enjoyed it too much."

I had, and the fight too. "I guess I'm all in," I admitted, more to myself than to him. It was the culmination of everything—overcoming the panic and fear, being here with my work, actually feeling a strong attraction that was about so much more than fulfilling my own needs.

I finally felt free. I saw no reason not to celebrate. I was much more a *tell me I can't do something, then stand back and watch me do it* person. And Meghan had delivered a challenge and it just so happened to be one I wanted to conquer. I hadn't let my past overwhelm me and keep me from doing this show. It wouldn't stop me from my end goal of sleeping with Lucas Caine.

One night, and he'd be out of my system.

One night to forget everything else existed.

One night to simply be me. Because no matter how bad my amnesia was, I'd always believed that my personality had always been this way.

"I can take you home, but I don't want to," Lucas said calmly.

"Do you always get what you want?"

His gaze fixed on me. "Don't you?"

I smiled a little and then I leaned in and let my kiss be my answer.

Nothing about tonight had been easy. Easy had never had a place in my life, and right now, I definitely didn't want it, not with his mouth insistently on mine, his body heat burning me as his hands traveled down to cup my ass in order to draw me against him more tightly.

I moaned into his mouth as the ache in my belly intensified. "I wanted to see the tattoos. All of them." I began to tug at his shirt which was already halfway undocked. His smile was pure bad boy, wicked intentions, and with a quick flick of his wrist the straps of my dress were off my shoulders and the fabric slid to a puddle at my feet.

I flushed at he stared with approval and lust in his expression. "Perfect."

"Not even close," I told him fiercely.

"Perfect for my intentions," he corrected and ran a hand across my lower back, pulling me against him. It felt strange to be naked against his mostly clothed body but it was also a turn-on. His cock pressed me through his pants. My body surged against his, my sex wet and hot and so ready for him.

His mouth on my nipple sent a series of shockwaves through me. He sucked hard, then bit lightly as his fingers slid between my legs and inside of me, setting me on edge, ready to detonate…explode.

I had zero control around Lucas. That fact alone overwhelmed me. Intense pleasure sliced through me as his mouth slid up my neck.

He reached between my legs, stroking me, smiling at the heat he found, because he knew it was for him. All of it.

One night, one night, one night, I sang inside my head. He would shatter me, and all I could do was urge him to do it faster, harder. The urgency that slammed us the moment we'd met had built to a nearly unbearable level—our time in the back room had barely taken the edge off, or maybe it amped us up more, furthering our anticipation to painfully frustrating levels.

My body laughed and shuddered as he thumbed my clit and the tight bundle of nerves vibrated through my entire body.

One night. Several orgasms, I amended as I sagged against him. But even in my post-orgasmic haze, I knew I still hadn't gotten my fill of seeing him. At the very least, I needed to satisfy my curiosity. Immediately.

"Please," I told him, tugging at his shirt.

"Now you think you're in charge?" he murmured with a small shake of his head. "Oh baby, it doesn't work that way. Not tonight, at least."

In response, I raked my nails along his sides. He shuddered, so I did it again.

"You want to see me that badly?"

"Yes, I have to."

He pulled the shirt off and for a long second, I just stared. The tattoos snaked their way around his biceps, ribbons of black and white and gray that complemented his muscles and the designs equally. I trailed a finger along one strand of tribal design that wrapped up around his shoulder and followed it around to his back.

Even in the soft shadows of his apartment, I

knew his backpiece was magnificent. It spanned his shoulders and the entire width of his back, and as I followed it with my eyes, he dropped his pants so I could see where the ink ended.

"You done?" he asked, without turning around.

Never. But my body needed more than a view, even though my sex spasmed at the sight of his naked self. "Beautiful," I murmured as I walked around him. I caught a glimpse of a small, one-sided smile from him and I went back to intently tracing his pecs, his ribcage and finally, I circled his nipples.

He hissed through his teeth, so I did it again.

And got the same effect.

There were also several scars that I didn't bother to stop and catalogue. There would be time later—I'd make sure of it.

"That's enough for now," he growled as he picked me up against him and carried me through the living room and into his bedroom. The window overlooked the city, and I watched him as he lay me out on his big bed. "Perfect. Perfect trouble," he added as he parted my legs with his body, palmed my thighs open and bent his head.

I didn't expect it when his tongue laved between my legs and I jolted and grabbed the sheets, the headboard, his hair, anywhere that might ground me when I was so obviously not. He was opening me, licking, exploring. Bringing me right to the precipice (again) in no time flat.

When I came, my legs stiffened, toes curling, cries escaping my throat. Sounds I didn't bother to hide. I couldn't have. I wasn't in control of my own body and I loved it.

He didn't push inside of me as much as he invaded me, his weight pressing me to the mattress, his thickness filling me, leaving me still for several moments while my body adjusted to the pure pleasure of just *having him*.

I rocked my hips up to match his motions, taking him in farther, enjoying the pinch of pain before the pleasure. Watching him take me, giving over that control, unable to stop the freight train of an orgasm that rushed through me.

In the middle of the night, I woke in a daze, unsure of where I was…until Lucas's body rustled next to mine. He kissed his way up my bare back and he took me in the moonlight that draped across the sheets, dappling our bare bodies as we knelt, my back to his chest.

It was perfect. Too much so. Painfully so, because I knew perfect wasn't built to last. It would blow away like the puffs of cotton from the wishing flowers I'd pick from the meadows upstate.

4

THE NEXT MORNING, I woke to find Lucas staring out the window, his bare back to me, jeans pulled on. When he turned, they weren't completely done up. His hair was tousled, the ink running over him, fascinating.

My heart beat uncomfortably fast. I wasn't done, could never be…but I *needed* to be. All the togetherness and warmth of last night was gone, replaced by the harsh light of reality. I was too close, too fast. There was danger all around, all around me and Lucas.

I was out of bed like a shot, gathering up my dress as I went.

"I've got some clothes for you in there," he called before I shut the door. And he'd in fact gotten me some brand-new fashion exercise-type clothes. And sneakers. All in the right sizes.

I yanked it all on, rather than do the walk of shame in my dress, then used his toothbrush. Hands through my hair for a quick, messy braid, a splash of water and soap to get rid of any traces of leftover makeup from last night and I was out of there.

When I headed directly toward Lucas's front door, he was standing near it, like he knew my plan...and he was holding my phone. "I programmed my number in your cell."

I grabbed it from him. "Presumptuous."

"Definitely. Use it."

I wouldn't. But I also didn't delete it. I told myself some bullshit about how it made me a stronger person by letting it sit there and tempt me...and I promised myself I'd erase it tomorrow. "Gotta go," I said in what I hoped was a breezy tone (although really, I was laughably far from the breezy type). "Thanks for the clothes."

His expression was of the *good luck to you* tongue-in-cheek variety, something I didn't relish at this moment. "Let me take you home. Or at least get you a cab. You're not prepared for what's out there."

Whatever it was had to be safer than him, so I didn't turn back, pushed past him. "I'm fine, really."

With my dress, bag and shoes all balled up, I

went out and down the stairs…and found myself in the face of two cameras with flashbulbs that burst into a thousand shattered pieces in front of my eyes and made me blink furiously. They sounded more like muffled bullets murdering my fledgling career than cameras whirring at the speed of light to invade my life and get this story. Whether Meghan tipped them off or they followed us here somehow—and really, when had I gotten that important?—it didn't matter. The damage was done—I was "out there."

There's no putting Ryn back in the box now.

I put my head down and walked until I could hail a cab. The photographers followed me the whole way, even running after the cab for a few minutes.

The cab driver barely glanced back at me, like this was a constant occurrence for him. "Where to?"

I gave my building's address. It was time to go home and face the music.

As I walked from the elevator to my door, I texted Brayden to let him know I was home safe—and that I was going to work. That wasn't all avoidance, because I was itching to draw and

I barely got through the door and punched the alarm code before I was grabbing for my supplies. I curled up on the couch before anything else could distract me, knowing I had to let it all out.

My emotions were all still wrapped up in Lucas and would be until I could release them, purge them, and forget them.

As if, a small, cynical part of me chided, which I ignored in favor of sweeping marks across the page with my eyes practically closed, remembering every inch of him. I let my confusion and leftover lust pour into the sketch, defining his biceps and lats and tattoos from memory, working feverishly, as though everything depended on it.

I sketched him in charcoal, his arms, his chest, bare back, what I could remember of the individual tattoos I tried to memorize while he slept. There were so many of them, intricately connected but obviously each a masterpiece unto itself. His biceps held more of the single pieces that were still connected by scrollwork, each tattoo a standout but yet managing to fade into a pattern.

I drew faster.

Skull.

Wings.

Dice.

Ace of spades.

I slowed when I got to his backpiece, an

intricate work in grayscale, masculine yet delicately exquisite. It reminded me of something, but like my memories, the harder I tried to grab it the slipperier it got.

When I was done, I was exhausted but nowhere near satiated. Far from exorcizing my desire for Lucas, it had only served to make it worse. Annoyed, I left the sketchbook on the kitchen table, put on a pot of coffee and then headed for the shower, so I could stop pretending the smell of Lucas wasn't driving me crazy.

When I came out, I dressed quickly in a T-shirt and leggings, but a strange sense washed over me, as if the energy in the apartment had been disturbed. The alarm was still armed, and after a quick check to make sure I was most definitely alone, I focused on the flowers. I'd registered them briefly when I'd first come in, a variety of vases gathered in the living room along the windowsill, and I'd assumed they'd been delivered to the gallery for me and brought here by Brayden.

Upon closer inspection, I noticed, among the other, more arranged bouquets, a small vase of daffodils that looked as if they'd come freshly picked, not from a flower shop. Even so, there was a small, white card with a typed message that simply read: *Great show.*

Unlike the others, this card was plain white

with no flower shop insignia. Maybe someone brought it to the gallery last night and Brayden dropped it by here. But could it be a coincidence that I'd found daffodils in here last night?

I jumped at the sudden, harsh sound of the buzzer, as someone pushed it intensely and several times in a row to get my attention. I quickly shoved the daffodils back so they were semi-buried behind the other flowers and went to the intercom.

Was it wrong that more than a small part of me was hoping it was Lucas? Ridiculous. I'd survived approximately twenty-four years without relying on a relationship and now, in just over twenty-four hours after meeting Lucas, I was unable to shake him from my brain.

An image flashed of him pinning me against the wall, followed quickly by one of me entangled in his sheets. Heat coursed through my body. I shook it off and pressed the intercom button.

"Ryn Taylor? This is Private Detective Dan Turner. I'm an investigator with the insurance company Brayden Hamilton hired to protect your art in his gallery."

I vaguely recalled Brayden mentioning Turner, back when my painting had first been stolen, but that was years ago. Why was he here now? And why for me? "Is there a problem?"

"It's an ongoing investigation, but I need to speak with you directly."

I hesitated but then buzzed him in. He wasn't technically law enforcement, but he also wasn't paparazzi and still I was a little—okay, *a lot*—unsettled about something I couldn't explain beyond a sudden random, bizarre fear of daffodils.

I waited for the knock on the door, more nervously than I would've liked to be. I tried to wipe that all away and wasn't sure I'd succeeded by the time I met Dan Turner, who in turn gave me the once-over before an almost sheepish smile emerged and he disarmed me with an apology.

"Sorry—your pictures don't do you justice."

"Neither do the articles," I informed him with a smile of my own.

Turner laughed appreciatively. I poured a cup of coffee and held it out to him. "That's great—thanks."

He didn't look anything like a man I'd associate with insurance agenting. He was tall and bulky, but not enough to look beefy. He reminded me of a boxer. He was good-looking in a rough sort of way, his brown eyes bordering on hazel in the sunlight splashing across my kitchen table where I'd motioned for him to sit.

"I didn't realize my stolen painting was still such a big deal," I admitted. "Not enough that they'd send someone out personally."

He nodded, as if he'd heard that before and explained, "Art and antiquities is a big business. Insurance companies take a lot of precautions so they don't take huge losses from theft or fire and especially from fraud, which is what happens in the majority of cases."

He wasn't telling me anything I didn't know—people did pretend that their priceless paintings had been stolen in order to collect millions… or they tried to, anyway. But that wasn't the case with my painting, so this still didn't make a lot of sense to me. "Was there a problem with any of the other paintings? Because Brayden didn't indicate anything…"

"Not at all, Ryn. I'm just getting close to tracking down your stolen painting, and I wanted the opportunity to talk to you."

"It's just that Brayden didn't mention this—"

Turner interrupted, "I don't have to run everything by him. Not when I'm investigating a painting that no doubt quadrupled in price overnight."

That last part should've been amazing news, and it was, but it also left me with a sudden pit in my stomach. Nothing in his demeanor changed, but the energy in the room did and I was uneasy again. He'd seemed friendly enough, but my unease was enough to make my inherent suspicions rise up—not having a memory left me open to the possibility that Dan Turner could be an enemy from my past. "I think maybe this meeting should happen with Brayden. I'm not sure I can be of any help to you at all."

He ignored that, pressed on with, "Do you have any theory about who stole your painting?"

"No."

"Brayden certainly knew what the value would become," he mused, almost as if he was only speaking to himself.

"I think it would be best if you spoke with Brayden. I wasn't in New York when the painting was stolen."

"To your knowledge, did it ever hang in the gallery or was it stolen in transit?"

"Not in transit," I replied. In truth, I knew exactly when and where but I didn't like fishing expeditions.

He stared at me, a frank assessment. "I heard there was quite a commotion at the show last night. And that Lucas Caine was in the middle of it all."

I simply shrugged. "It's a blur."

"I can imagine, what with it being your first real show." He paused. "Have you had any problems with stalkers?"

Images of the daffodils flashed before my eyes. "No."

"Are you sure? Maybe you haven't realized it yet, since you're more like, what did Meghan call you, 'feral Nell'? I guess she meant that you're not used to being out and about."

Megan's words burned through me the way they had last night. "I live in a doorman building. I'm with Brayden the majority of the time when I go out, so I think I'd notice."

Turner was looking at the open sketchbook that I'd left on the kitchen counter. He wouldn't know the sketch was Lucas unless he knew about the tattoos. But really, a lot of men had a lot of tattoos.

He removed all doubt with his next comments. "Nice work. Interesting company you're keeping."

"Why is that your business?"

"You made it everyone's business—it's in all the papers."

"Really? *All* of them?" I managed dryly. "I think you should definitely speak to Brayden about all of this and not me." I flipped the sketchbook closed and tucked the pad protectively under my arm. "I've got a lot to do."

"Have the police been by to speak with you?"

"Police?" I asked, confused.

"Rumor is that Meghan VanValen is pressing

charges." He gave a small wince. "But I'm betting you don't deal in rumors."

There was no good way to answer that. "Why are you keeping track of my life?" I demanded. "I didn't steal my own painting."

"You have no idea how many times I've heard an artist or dealer lie to me about that," Turner said calmly. "I'll be back, Ryn. In the meantime, you might want to reconsider your current associations." He paused. "By the way, I couldn't find an address on you prior to the Catskills."

"What does that have to do with your investigation?"

"Maybe nothing. Maybe everything," he said, and I hated him.

"Please leave. Now."

He took his time, finished the coffee I'd poured. I resisted the urge to snatch the mug from him and throw it—either at him or against the wall—but since rumor had it I might be getting a police visit, I figured I needed to keep the assault and battery to a minimum. Finally, he went to the door and let himself out, but not before he called over his shoulder, "Watch out for Lucas Caine. Trust me on that—he's not the type of man you want in your life."

I didn't want to tell him that maybe Lucas Caine should be the one watching out for me.

I was shaken. I locked the doors and stared at the goddamned daffodils. Dan Turner was up to something—Brayden should've warned me, dammit.

I stopped myself from firing off a snotty text. Instead, I went into the studio room and painted until the sun went down. Until my eyelids got heavy, and earlier than they normally would've. I blamed the stress of last night, of the last weeks, and I curled in bed and closed my eyes.

In what seemed like seconds, I was awake, staring up at a dreary gray sky. I blinked, and my mouth opened to a silent scream but those were the only motions I could accomplish. My body was otherwise paralyzed, slowly being covered in daffodils that kept falling on me, drifting in like a fat, steady rain.

By the time I realized I was lying in an open grave being slowly buried alive by the flowers, I did scream out loud and woke myself up.

Still shaking, the first thing I did was carry the vase with the daffodils out to the trash room and threw the vase down the chute. Satisfied, I went back into my apartment and locked the door behind me.

The second thing I did was call Lucas. He answered halfway through the second ring, sounding out of breath. I closed my eyes, mortified that I might've caught him in the middle of having sex. More mortified at the thought that he'd picked up. "I'm sorry—I didn't mean to bother you," I choked out.

"Couldn't sleep. I'm out for a run," he huffed.

My body sagged in stupid relief. Silly, foolish girl. "It's three in the morning."

"What's your point?"

"I want to run with you."

"Then get dressed. I'll ring in nine minutes."

"I'll meet you downstairs." When I looked at the clock, I noted I'd only been asleep for a couple of hours. I pulled my hair into a messy bun and slid into jogging capris and a tank top. I put my sneakers on in the elevator. I was walking down the front hall when Lucas came into the building.

The locked building.

"Doorman," he said when I opened my mouth to ask how he got in, but I chose to accept that. I couldn't deny there was a certain excitement—and comfort—that Lucas could get to me at anytime.

We walked a few minutes—he'd already warmed up so I picked up my pace. I knew he was jogging slower for me, so I pushed hard and it felt good. I lost myself in the rhythm of my feet on the pavement, the blur of the shadowed surroundings, the sounds of the city instead of my usual music blaring from my iPod's earbuds.

I'd noticed him looking over his shoulder, but it took me a while. When he noticed me noticing, he stopped. But I'd felt it too, that overly paranoid *I'm being followed* sixth sense.

I had no idea how long we ran for, but it was long and hard enough to make my muscles tremble when I finally slowed. My mind was clear, almost dizzy, and it had been exactly what I needed.

We both slowed to a walk, not speaking still. As if in tune, we ended up in front of my building. In the elevator, I turned to him and kissed him. Wordlessly, he carried me into my apartment, never letting me down, only stopping the kiss to get the key inside the lock. I didn't stop, sucked on his neck, nipping, marking, hearing the growl vibrate in his throat as I did so.

I wondered briefly if he could go into work with hickeys on his neck, but it was too late to worry. My emotions were running overboard, and the running took the edge off, but it wasn't enough. I shoved him to the wall, and he let me pin him.

We were like two insatiable teenagers with some kind of crazy, forbidden love who couldn't get enough of each other. His mouth, hot on mine, slick skin sliding together. His hand between my legs. Caught between exposed and orgasm and not caring, only wanting to reach that place with him where nothing else mattered.

Sharing a run with him felt more intimate than sex, or at least I felt more vulnerable. Normally, I was able to distance myself during sex, but I'd already realized that none of my normal defense mechanisms worked with Lucas Caine.

If I wanted to outrun him, I'd have to try a lot harder.

In the aftermath, we remained entwined, my back against the wall, his weight on me.

He lifted his head from where it had been buried against my neck to note wryly, "You remind me of me."

"Is that good or bad?"

"I haven't figured that out."

Impulsively, I reached up and stroked his cheek. He looked surprised, but definitely not unhappy. "What if I hadn't called you?"

"Why do you think I was out running at three in the morning? It was either that or end up at your door."

"But you're here anyway."

"I was invited," he murmured, but now I knew he would've shown up anyway. I shivered, partly at his words, but Lucas frowned. "We need to get you into the shower."

Reluctantly, we untangled from each other. Naked, with his gaze lingering on me, I put on fresh coffee then went to start the shower. When I went back out to get him, he was turning the business card Turner had left on the counter over and over between his fingers.

Now, he asked, "Why was this guy here?"

"You know him?" I asked and he nodded. "He's with Brayden's insurance company for the gallery. He's investigating a stolen painting of mine. He said it went up in value..." I trailed off. "He was an asshole."

Lucas gave a faint smile. "Let Brayden take care of the business shit—that's why he gets a commission."

I nodded, then frowned, reminded again about last night. "Turner said that my fight was in all the papers. And that Meghan talked to reporters about suing me."

"Meghan didn't talk to reporters. Ann Maslow caught the end of the fight."

"How lucky of her, the fucking stalker."

He laughed. "You give her something to talk about, she's going to talk, Ryn. A simple formula."

Nothing about that was simple but what was in front of me: naked man, willing women, warm shower beckoning.

I chose wisely.

5

"I FIGURED I'D GIVE you some space, but enough's enough," Brayden announced. At least he'd come bearing food. And coffee. And no recriminations from the night before last. Just the opposite, in fact. "Your show was a huge success, love."

It was an hour since Lucas had left, murmuring something about meetings. When Brayden set down the extra-large coffee in front of me, I admitted, "I thought you'd be angry."

"First of all, I was worried," he said. "But I knew you were in good hands and babe, I knew it sucked, but you sold double after you lost your shit."

I sighed. "Great. Even if they doubted it before, now everyone knows I'm imbalanced."

"Everyone knows they shouldn't fuck with

you. It's an oddly compelling selling point. I've got people who want special orders."

It took a long, pre-caffeinated moment for that to sink in. "Wait, I'm being commissioned?"

Brayden smiled. "So you do listen when I talk."

I swatted him on the arm and grabbed for a bagel. I inhaled the soft, warm bread and cream cheese, realizing that I hadn't eaten since yesterday morning. "Details. I need details."

His words were cautious, but he couldn't hide his excitement. "Mystery buyer. Wealthy, of course. He wants a series of paintings, based on photos." I hesitated and he continued, "You've never done that, I know, but for half a million…"

"I swear my heart just stopped."

He grinned, then sobered. "I'm going to make sure you're taken care of, baby girl. The money's cool, but being commissioned is a good career step." He reached out and squeezed my hand. "So I told him, trial basis. Give me one picture, no promises."

I blew out a breath of relief. "What would I do without you, Bray?"

"You won't have to find out." He paused. "The pictures are normal. I already checked them out."

"Normal."

"No people. No faces. No beach."

"Okay. So what is it?"

"It's a house." He showed me the photo of an innocuous but beautiful house with the ocean behind it that might've been found in any beach community in this country. I stared at it, with no weird feelings whatsoever accompanying my gaze. In fact, the whole thing looked really... boring. "Okay, I'll give it a try."

"A try? For this money, Ryn—"

I held up my hand. "Temperamental artist, remember?"

"Can't forget even if I tried. Promise." He glanced at the bed. "Up all night working?"

I could've lied, but why start now? "I saw Lucas."

"Again?"

"Yes."

Brayden gave a small frown. "He called you?"

"I called him. At three in the morning. We went for a run...and then..."

He held up his hand. "I don't need the details." After a small pause, he said, "He must've freaked when you ran out on him the morning after the show."

"How do you know I ran out on him?"

He gave me a meaningful look that reminded me of just how well he knew me and capped it with, "You're such a guy sometimes."

"I'm sure I'm just a convenient piece of ass."

"Baby girl, you're not convenient at all," Brayden assured me.

"What's that supposed to mean?"

"You outmaneuvered him without even trying, so of course that means you two will end up chasing each other all around the goddamned city."

"I don't want that," I insisted. I already had a dark past I couldn't remember. I shouldn't be involved with a dangerous man like Lucas, no matter how badly my body wanted him. Nice guys liked me, and I tried with them, I truly did. But I tended to walk over them. I needed someone stronger. Someone who wouldn't put up with my shit.

Someone who let me run, who gave me just enough rope to tangle myself up in...someone who enjoyed the challenge as much as they challenged me.

"So, you're thinking one-night stand?" Brayden asked. "Because it's already been two nights."

"Same thing." I shrugged. "You said yourself that Lucas isn't into long term. He's more the conquer and move on type."

Brayden smiled. "I thought that was you."

I nudged him. "I learned from the best. And hey, it'll give Ann Maslow more to write about when Lucas moves on to his next conquest."

"Or when you do. And hey, all press is good press. I stand by that. But for the time being, I'm banning art magazines and gossip columns from your place."

"Smart move."

Brayden's gaze flicked over mine. "You've got to realize that you're as much of a mystery to him as he is to you."

"Maybe."

"Definitely," Brayden asserted. "All I can tell you is that he's dark. And he's not the kind of guy you want to be involved with."

"I didn't say I wanted to be"—air quotes—"*involved*."

"Good. Except you're lying."

"Shut up," I muttered. I had other things to worry about, like the fact that I was losing my mind. I'd thrown out the vase of flowers, but when I'd checked the garbage this morning, it had been empty of the daffodils I'd thrown out the night before the show. Either Brayden was acting as full-time butler or else I'd dreamed the spill. And I knew I hadn't taken my meds that night, but as of this morning, two were missing.

I was always careful. I wrote down when I took the pills and I never, ever took two pills at once.

God, was I going crazy? Had I *been* crazy at one point?

I rubbed the light scars that ran behind my ears. I had a new face—did I somehow have a new personality too? Was my old self breaking through?

Your eyes will always be the same, Brayden would tell me when I went through periods of doubt like this. *You can't hide from them—they'll tell you who you are.*

Brayden had wisely dropped the subject of me and Lucas. But I realized that was because something else had caught his attention. Dan Turner's business card was still on the counter—it had taken Brayden only slightly longer than it had Lucas to notice it, forget whatever else he was talking about and frown in my direction.

"Turner came here yesterday," I began. "He said he was tracking new leads on my stolen painting."

There was no mistaking the sarcasm in his "Really?"

"He implied that because the demand got higher after your show the insurance company renewed their search."

Brayden snorted. "Right."

"Did you know any of that?"

"I didn't know Turner would be coming to question you—I'll make sure it doesn't happen again," Brayden said, sidestepping the question.

I tried again with a different approach. "How

much money are my paintings suddenly worth?"

Brayden gave a smile—a small one, and I suddenly knew exactly what was meant by treating triumph and tragedy as the same impostor. I shouldn't worry about money and success. I never had. I'd let Brayden do it, trusted him and Susan and a lawyer who'd been set up separately to look after all my interests, all so I could do what I loved unencumbered.

"I've seen it," Brayden told me now without me having to say a word. "An artist gets caught up in chasing the fame. It's not even the money most of the time, it's the fame. And from there, it's really easy to lose the gifts you were given. I don't ever want to see that happen to you."

He looked so heartbroken when he talked about it. That, and the casual way he dressed this morning, made me think about his past. His flannel shirt was opened and gray sweats and bare feet was a good look on him. He looked like a college kid, not a business owner, and I didn't have to wonder why he always dressed in suits when he went out. His suit of armor, he called it, different than how he'd spent time from ages fifteen to twenty. He didn't talk much about that time. I know he lived on the streets and he told me he did what he had to in order to survive. I could only imagine what that entailed.

I dropped that subject and veered off onto another uncomfortable one. "Should I ask how bad the news is surrounding the show, or at least ask about the reviews?"

Brayden shot me a "Do you really want to know" look. And I didn't, but I also didn't want others to know things about me they could use as darts to sling at me. "The competition's cutthroat, Ryn. You'll find out they'll use anything against you."

"There's nothing to know."

But I was lying—in truth, what Brayden told me shook me. Suppose something from my past was there, right in front of my face? It was one thing for the competition to plant stories about me, but I couldn't defend myself against what I didn't know.

"Ryn, I won't let anything happen to you," Brayden told me. "No one's going to use you."

"I don't think Lucas is," I said.

Judging by the look on Brayden's face, he wasn't accepting that easily at all.

Later that night I had the dream, the one I'd started having nightly after I'd woken up in the hospital post-memory loss. It was rare for me to have it these days, probably because the contents of it were never far from my waking thoughts.

I stand on the beach in the dark. My toes curl in the cold sand. The scent of salty high tide is still on my skin to compete with the dank smell of ocean that wafts over me. The roar of the waves seems loud enough to drown out all other sounds. Except it doesn't.

Voices.

Shadowed figures.

Gunshots.

I scream, loud enough to be heard over the crashing water.

I scream in real life too, loud enough to no doubt wake the neighbors, so I force myself to stop, swallow the yells as I blink myself fully awake. I'm bathed in sweat and breathing hard. I stumble to the bathroom and splash water on my face. I catch sight of myself in the mirror. I look wild-eyed.

It took me the better part of an hour, and a few shots of whiskey, to calm myself down sufficiently enough. I wrapped myself in a blanket on the couch, thankful that I didn't find any errant flowers lying around. That was a bright spot.

Even so, I had to force myself not to call Lucas. *No more of that*, I told myself firmly. I could get through this all by myself.

Finally, I felt better. I'd stopped shaking. So I went into my studio to study the night's work, to see if anything there might've triggered my dream.

Before I'd slept, I'd finished the first try at the painting I'd been commissioned to draw. The house in the photo was plain. Nondescript. And I'd been fine sketching it out. Perhaps my first drawing was a little uninspired, but I was sure that didn't show. And I'd managed to do a little more than a straightforward rendering. I'd blended and shaded. Made it look more art than photo.

And if the man who'd commissioned it didn't want it, so be it, I'd told myself. And then I'd gotten down to the actual painting of the house, ignoring my own inner critic, and anything else that threatened to get in my way. I forced all of it out of my mind ruthlessly, like I did with anything that could fuck with my art.

Under the harsh morning light, I studied yesterday's pieces and wondered if maybe the dream was all about the risk of trying something new. Dr. B had warned me that change—even and especially good change—was high on the list of stresses.

This picture seemed to underscore that. The dark slashes of color undercut what would've been a conventionally pleasing picture. A beach, a wash of water foaming the shore…the skyline of a storm rolling in, but a sinister one. I even shivered when I looked at it, as though the icy rain was cutting my skin.

Disturbingly beautiful. I could hear the critics now. But there was more to it. All of my paintings separately meant nothing. Put together, there was a pattern that I had yet to discern.

I had the book, my portfolio, kept painstakingly by Brayden. Pictures of each and every piece I'd sold. I flipped through them with a growing sense of dread.

What the hell happened to me?

I'd been on my own with an ID from the time I was seventeen, and I'd walked into that café with my new social security number and it hadn't triggered any manhunts or arrest records.

I was running. I knew that. From who, I couldn't remember.

6

I DIDN'T HEAR FROM Lucas for three days, but I didn't notice, because I'd been locked inside my own world, *painting my ass off*, as Brayden put it. I'd put aside the commissioned work, wary of having that dream again, but mainly it was because I'd been inspired by other things.

Like Lucas. More than I'd like to admit.

But then three days turned into a week that turned into two weeks and that lack of contact, I most definitely noticed. At first I was fine, and then I was upset, and then I was angry at myself for being upset. And then I was just angry. I'd gone a long time without letting a guy do this to me. I'd promised myself I'd be the one who walked away without a look back, and I had been...until the run, dammit. He'd pulled me back when he'd answered my distress call at three in the morning, just when I'd needed him most.

Bastard. Of course, I hadn't reached out to call him either, so we had a big game of chicken going on. Or maybe that was only happening in my own head.

Even though I didn't specifically talk about this with Brayden in these terms, he was good about not saying "I told you so." Instead, he took me out, brought me shopping and to dinner and made sure he fueled my art-driven rages.

When I came up for air after the last one, I realized that I'd effectively channeled the hurt and deception into what might be my best work ever. I'd closed the curtains on the city landscape and pictured my beloved woods instead. And when that hadn't worked, I'd gotten in the car and drove the three hours to the place that was still mine. My landlady knew my car, so I wasn't worried about scaring her, despite the fact it was one in the morning.

And finally, everything stilled. I didn't feel the man in the woods there the way I had in the past, not until four in the morning. And finally I was able to paint the way I needed to.

I slept most of the morning, until I couldn't ignore Brayden's incessant phone calls, reminding me of the event he'd committed me to. "Is that tonight?" I groaned. "You barely gave me any notice."

He had the nerve to sound amused when he said, "I told you about it two weeks ago. Come home now. All you've got to do is be showered by six and I'll have everything else taken care of."

I grumbled, but did as he asked. Sort of. I was home by the time Brayden and his glam squad showed at the door. I smiled, and they looked at me, horrified. Probably because I was covered in paint.

Brayden steered me toward the bathroom by the elbow, muttering, "I told you to shower by six."

"I did," I said defensively. "And then I started working again on the commissioned piece."

He stopped, rolled his eyes, because he knew he couldn't argue about a painting that was bringing in that much money, and turned to the two women armed with curling irons and makeup. "Do the best you can. Her hair's still damp so the paint should come out easily. Otherwise, make it look like highlights. Or something." Reluctantly, I sat and let them primp me. Brayden had picked out a dress that I ended up loving, although he refused to tell me where we were going with a definitive other than, "You'll see."

Which meant I was going to hate it.

Brayden called me on my attitude when we got into the car. "Don't get pissy with me because you still haven't heard from Lucas."

"How do you know I haven't heard from him?" I huffed.

He just snorted and handed me a glass of champagne as the limo pulled into the New York city night's traffic. "He's not the kind to keep in touch. We both know the type. We are the type." He softened then. "He's busy. And so are you, right?"

I had to agree. I sat back in the air-conditioned comfort and watched the city slowly roll by. Traffic was always more of a bitch during September, Brayden had warned me, and even though we were only going ten blocks, it would take forty minutes during rush hour.

Finally, we pulled up into a line of limos and I craned to look down the street. There was a red carpet with a step and repeat, tons of photographers and a line of limos around the block. Although yesterday had been a beautifully crisp fall day, today had been closer to sweltering. It was a humid seventy-five degrees and people were rushing to get inside the building and into the air conditioning. I didn't want to leave the car. "This looks like a big event."

"It's for charity," Brayden told me.

"Why are we here?"

"You don't want to do anything charitable?" he

asked innocently.

"You've got an angle, Bray."

He didn't argue. "We're here to rehabilitate your image and make you out to be a productive member of society."

"Nice try."

Brayden smirked. "A little charity work goes a long way. Besides, the crazy artist who's sleeping with Lucas and punching out his ex-girlfriends and reporters at her shows is a big draw."

"I didn't punch anyone out. Not any reporters," I corrected. It was my first appearance at an event since my own show...other than being caught coming out of Lucas's apartment. Now, I side-eyed Brayden. "What's the catch?"

"You're up for auction."

I groaned. "Like as a date?"

"Don't be silly," he scoffed. "You're too unstable for them to even consider that."

"Asshole," I said in a singsong voice even as my anxiety rose.

"You're donating a portrait session."

My heartbeat slowed slightly. "That's not so bad."

"And it needs to be completed by the end of the week."

"As in *Friday*? As in tomorrow is *Friday* Friday?" I asked, my voice rising with each word.

"All the artists who donated agreed to those terms so the portraits can be displayed at the charity's annual awards dinner. Which is held next week."

Great. Nothing like forced creativity. "I think you suck," I said through my teeth, since we'd entered what appeared to me as a glorified gauntlet.

"Just hang on to me." His grip tightened around mine. "And I'm not letting you out of my sight."

"God, this is awful," I murmured as several members of the board—according to Brayden's barely-there whisperings—descended on us. I heard a few of the photographers ask me if Lucas was coming, and neither Brayden nor I engaged them. A few asked me if I was planning on getting into another fight that night, and of course, I ignored that question too.

"Just smile and follow my lead. You're not leaving my side," Brayden assured me. "We only need to stay through the auction."

Flashbulbs popped and I wondered if Lucas might make a surprise appearance tonight. That would be just like him.

As if you know him so well, I chided myself. But I did. And that's what worried me the most.

I was halfway hoping to see him here. Instead, I spotted Meghan, and it was definitely not an equal trade. Nor a pleasant one.

Of course, people noticed that we were in a room together and were probably hoping for another fight. But I wouldn't make the same mistake twice of letting her get to me.

"You're doing great," Brayden said to me as he scanned the room.

"I'm trying. Anyone here for you?"

"There's always someone here for me." Brayden had always taken advantage of being good-looking and single, a combination that got him laid consistently.

He'd never wanted to be tied down. And even though I wanted him to have someone in his life who loved him, I'd realized that he did. That was me. And vice versa.

"Whatever happened to that guy you were seeing?"

"Zack?" He shrugged. "He's still around."

"Wait, so you've seen him more than once?"

"I *see* a lot of guys more than once. But that's as far as it goes."

I'd adopted my attitude about keeping things light from him, because it worked so well for him. At least it had...until Lucas.

To distract myself from that thought, I had some passed hors d'oeuvres, made some small talk and concentrated on getting through this alive.

When the auction began, there were several artists I recognized through the magazines Brayden had around his apartment and the gallery, and others whose names I knew because of their artwork. It was an eclectic group and the first five artists got great bids.

Of course, now I was panicked that no one would bid on me. "Bray, if no one bids—"

"I've got you covered," he assured me, even as the auctioneer called me up to the stage. I didn't have time to think about refusing, because Brayden took me in hand, escorted me up the few stairs and gave me a subtle push the final way up to the stage. When the auctioneer read my bio out loud, I shifted uncomfortably. I wasn't used to eyes on me. On my art, fine.

I stared out into the crowd, the faces swimming in front of me. No one looked friendly. It was too quiet out there, and my mind started going places it shouldn't. I willed myself not to have a panic attack.

Thankfully, the bidding began quickly, and I was surprised to see so many hands go up from the start. After several minutes, it boiled down between two buyers, both women. One of them was an older woman, and the other?

Was Meghan.

Yes, *that* Meghan. I wanted to turn to the

auctioneer and tell him to just take the older woman's bid and I'd pay the difference, but of course, the universe doesn't work that way.

"Going once, going twice…a Ryn Taylor private portrait session sold to Miss Meghan VanValen."

And that announcement in and of itself caused a nice stir among the audience. So much for rehabilitating my image. I was definitely killing Brayden tonight. Or at least strangling him.

Except by the time I left the stage and went back to our table where my purse was, Brayden was gone.

"Your boyfriend said the limo's waiting to take you home," one of the women we'd been sitting near told me. "I was watching your bag."

I didn't bother correcting the boyfriend part, instead smiling with a quick, "Great, thanks," and I was out of there before the small-talk-aperitif section of the party began. I'd done my duty and now I was stuck dealing with Meghan.

Tomorrow.

At least Brayden had left me the car, but not a text telling me what happened to him. I texted him a quick, *Are you okay?* and got a fast, *Yes, sorry—talk tomorrow.*

After the crap I'd pulled at my own gallery show, I had no right to be angry. If he had to leave, it couldn't be helped.

I got home quickly, without incident, my mind still wrapped up in how exactly I was going to handle spending more time with Meghan tomorrow while I unzipped my dress and shrugged out of it. The easiest way to get rid of all the makeup was to shower, especially since my cleavage and arms had been dusted with some kind of shimmer powder. So I let the hot water erase the tension that had set in hard from the moment Meghan had begun bidding on me, and tried to let some creativity creep its way in.

Tomorrow, I'd paint her. She'd be effectively baring her soul to me—did she not get that? Why would she open herself up to her perceived enemy that way?

I'd dried off and thrown a long T-shirt on when my cell buzzed. It was after midnight, which meant it could be Brayden. Or…

Lucas. I debated not answering for the briefest of seconds, but considering how long I'd been waiting to hear from him, that would be foolish.

"Hey," I said softly.

"Hey," he echoed. He sounded far away. Tired.

I was immediately concerned, and any anger I'd held toward him melted, replaced with anger at myself. Why hadn't I checked in with him? He'd literally come running last time I'd called. "Are you all right?"

"I will be." He paused. "Better now, hearing your voice."

"Are you home?"

"Almost. By tomorrow night."

"Come see me then." It was more than a request, a demand, really, but he didn't seem to mind.

"Definitely. How's work going tonight? I'm interrupting."

"No, I didn't start yet." I glanced over toward the room where the supplies were, then settled on the couch instead.

"Don't want to keep you."

"You're not," I promised.

It sounded like he was someplace quiet. I didn't hear sounds of TV or traffic. And despite the tiredness in his tone, he was also oddly alert. "Your doors and windows locked?"

"Yes."

"Alarmed?"

"Yes."

"You're not running late without me, right?"

His questions were protective, and it felt much nicer than I'd expected and not at all smothering. "No."

"Good."

I thought about telling him about Meghan, but I considered how it might hurt him. I felt that's what Meghan wanted to do, to him and to me, to drive a wedge between us…and I was determined to not be the person in Lucas's life who hurt him. "You couldn't sleep."

"I never sleep well," he admitted. "After a while, necessity becomes habit."

"Have you always been a night person? I mean, I assume you are because you were running at three in the morning."

"Born that way," he agreed. "I've always had trouble going to sleep at a supposedly normal time. When I was school-aged, maybe eight or nine, I'd climb out onto the roof and sleep under the sky. My room was small and claustrophobic, and I was always too hot, like my skin didn't fit. I told my school counselor that once."

"I can't see that going over well."

"It didn't. I learned to keep my mouth shut and just do what I wanted. A 'safer to ask for forgiveness than permission' kind of thing."

"Funny, but I can't see you doing either."

"Were you ever a school counselor?" he deadpanned.

I couldn't help but laugh. Even so, I couldn't get the image of him sleeping alone on a roof at seven, eight and nine out of my mind. "Do you still sleep outside?"

"I prefer the comforts of a bed, as long as I've

got a big enough room. I outgrew a lot of things."

"But you never forgot," I murmured, more to myself than him.

"Do you paint to forget?" he asked.

I painted because I couldn't remember, so technically that wasn't the same thing at all. "No. To immortalize."

"The plight of all great artists—to leave something of themselves behind," he said softly.

"I never think of myself as great." I never thought of myself in terms of my talent at all. It didn't work that way for me.

"Have you always painted?"

"Yes," I said firmly. It was always the answer in the forefront of my mind. Right or wrong, I felt it was the correct one.

"I should let you get on with your work," he said.

I didn't want the conversation to end. I had so many more questions, about his childhood, his job…but my questions would breed questions about my own childhood, and I wasn't ready for that. "Tomorrow," I reminded him.

"Tomorrow," he told me firmly.

Brayden showed at my door the next morning

with breakfast and more importantly, coffee, but with no real explanation of where he'd gone to last night. Instead, he laid out the food on my kitchen island while I tucked my legs under me on one of the stools and sipped the hot, strong coffee with one shot and foamed milk and immediately forgave him.

"Lucas called last night," I started. Brayden's brows rose. "I didn't tell him about the auction."

"It was getting tense with the bidding when I left," he offered.

"You didn't see who won?"

He gave a rueful smile. "Meghan already called the gallery with a time and place. That's why I'm here—to caffeinate you and deliver you to her within the hour."

I took back my feelings of forgiveness immediately. "I should never have agreed to this auction," I moaned, feeling very sorry for myself.

"Definitely not," Brayden agreed.

"You're the idiot who made me to do it."

"Since when did you start listening to me?"

"I should've known it was a trap. Maybe she'll agree to a gag."

"Kinky."

I threw my napkin at him and wondered if Meghan would've had the balls to bid if Lucas had been there? And if Lucas knew, would he stop the portrait session? Pay Meghan off so I could get out of it?

No, I had to deal with this myself, mainly because that last thought annoyed me. I didn't want Lucas to run my entire life. Granted, it made things easier, but I refused to get used to it. He could be gone in a flash. He'd already disappeared for weeks, and I was still annoyed that I'd allowed myself to care.

"Where am I meeting her highness?" I asked.

"At my suggestion, at the gallery, in the back room. It's safer for you to be around other people, like my assistant."

I agreed, then paused. "Wait, did she suggest the back room?"

Brayden frowned slightly. "Actually, she did."

I groaned. "Suppose she wants a nude?"

"She wouldn't," he scoffed.

She did—a "partial, tasteful nude," Meghan emphasized through her perfectly nude pouted lips, then shrugged out of her dress in one lithe move, calculatedly naked underneath. Casually, she bent down to pick up the material, smoothing it out over the back of the nearest chair before kicking off her heels and settling onto the upholstered bench without a hint of self-consciousness.

She didn't have a reason to be. I couldn't find a flaw and trust me, I wanted to. But today, I was being paid to be the artist with a cool, critical eye. I appraised her the way I imagined Ann Maslow did a perfect piece of artwork.

From an objective point of view, she was beautiful. Technically, at least, which to me always translated as cold, even though I tried to be objective. Part of it was because I couldn't stand her, but I'd be damned if I let that screw up my artwork. That was all I needed, to have her show off work that wasn't my best.

No, I was going to really see her, no matter if it killed me.

I studied her for a while.

Perfection in and of itself could be really boring. Part jealous bitch and part truth-teller. I needed to find an odd angle, a shadow, an imperfection….something to focus on or else this portrait would look boring as fuck.

Perfect didn't translate well to the canvas, and the canvas would hold my name.

Her legs were curled partially under her, breasts bared unselfconsciously, long neck graceful in the morning sunshine. Brayden's assistant, Suki, had placed the bench by the window with the most light pouring down on it earlier before giving me a glance that was all apology.

"Is this position okay?" Meghan asked finally, fishing for a spoken compliment, even though I know I'd given her enough with my facial expression.

Brayden always told me to never play poker… at least not for money. "Strip poker's probably okay," he'd joked.

"The bench placement is fine. Not sure of your position just yet." *Where are your flaws, Meghan? Show them to me. Come out, come out wherever you are…*

Meghan sighed, unappreciative of the work she couldn't yet see. She was already antsy. "You're not surprised I bid."

"Not really. Maybe a little."

She sighed. "This was probably a mistake."

Really? Or was this persona a calculated move? "We'll make it work."

Her eyes locked on mine. "Why would you do that?"

I tilted my head and stared at her. She wouldn't be my BFF. Maybe she'd hate the portrait, but I wouldn't. I was going to create something that would reveal her, something I would always be proud of.

I made art. Sometimes it revealed the ugly side

of life, but the art itself was never inherently ugly.

But I didn't tell her any of that. Instead, I skimmed over her question and said, "The pose isn't working. It's been done a thousand times. Let's try for different."

She narrowed her eyes at me, unsure of whether or not she could trust me. "What are you thinking?"

"Something less perfect," I said honestly. "You might have to get dirty. Literally."

Surprisingly, she didn't object. For the next ten minutes, she sat and waited for me to give the next directions, which included me "painting" her, with Suki's help, with a mixture of brown paint watered down just enough to look like dirt. We moved the bench and threw down a drop cloth.

It was far less Playboy bunny than her first pose and somehow way more seductive—at least I thought so, and I was pretty sure most red-blooded males who liked women would agree. This was dirty-sexy-hot, and Meghan actually seemed to enjoy it. Even her smile was wicked but not practiced…there was something of a teenage rebellion-freedom thing happening and I cranked up some classic rock as I sketched and lost track of time.

"Lucas is a very complicated man. I don't think in all those years I ever even scratched the surface," Meghan started, out of the blue, and I was trapped. I just wanted to paint and finish, but I wasn't even close to being done, and if I walked now, I'd have to start all over again.

I glanced up at her, acknowledging that I'd let her talk, then went back to shading my initial sketch. Her skin was even more gorgeous in the morning light, almost luminous, especially since her look today was very natural.

"He needed me so badly at one point. I helped him through a difficult period. I was there for him, and after he used me to heal, he was gone."

I wanted to tell her that Lucas wasn't healed at all, but I bit my tongue.

"He makes you think he'll be there. That he's never felt like this. He makes you fall for him and then he backs off like you're trying to trap him."

"You can't keep someone who doesn't want to stay," I said finally, and with a great deal of caution. "And why would you want that? You don't deserve that—you deserve someone who'll be there wholeheartedly." She looked surprised that I'd spoken at all, but I wasn't done. "I had nothing to do with coming between you and Lucas."

"I know that. I'm not stupid."

"No, you're stuck." I motioned. "Leg forward please."

She did as I asked and I painted in blissful

silence for several hours. In my mind, I labeled her painting *Fierceness and Fear* because those two emotions fought for dominance in her expression. In the end, I'd shadowed half her face and changed that expression slightly, as if she wore two masks at once. She stared out at a point over my shoulder, tears threatening but never falling, looking beautiful in her vulnerability.

I didn't kid myself about this fragile truce—if anything, she'd hate me more after this, especially after she saw the painting. This whole commissioning would do the opposite of what she'd intended. I'd know her far too well, and she'd hate me for it…if she didn't already.

I'D STAYED AT THE gallery late, finishing up the final touches on Meghan's painting. Brayden's assistant texted a picture of the finished piece to Meghan and assured her that it would be delivered in the morning to allow the paint to dry further. Meghan had been agreeable to that and I was definitely mentally exhausted and totally fucked up from the entire experience. Maybe Meghan *had* known what she was doing. Maybe I *was* the stupid one. Add to that, I'd learned from my doorman that Turner had tried to pay me a visit earlier that day and I'd been spinning by the time I'd reached my door.

The bright spot—and what had allowed me to fall into a deep sleep almost immediately upon letting myself into to my apartment—had been discovering that, while some of the flowers from the night of my show were starting to turn and others were blooming strong, there were no new additions. No daffodils.

Now, my sleep was unmercifully interrupted. I grabbed for my ringing cell phone, reaching blindly for it in the soft couch cushions I'd sunk into and could only manage to answer with "Yeah?"

"I woke you."

"Yes." Even so, Lucas's voice was definitely not unwelcome. I blinked and glanced over at the clock on the cable box, noted it was close to eleven and realized just as fast that I was suddenly starving. "I hope you're calling to offer dinner."

Lucas's laugh was easy. "If that's what you want. You up for going out?"

I sat up and tried to shake off the remnants of sleep. "What's serving now, beyond a diner?"

"Ryn, you have no idea. Pick you up in twenty." He hung up and I got myself showered and dressed. I wore an easy, spaghetti strap maxi-dress, figuring that I didn't need to do more than dress comfortably for a midnight supper. Even so, I threw on a moto jacket and a cute fringe bag and put on a light dusting of the shimmer makeup that made my eyes look huge. My hair hung straight and heavy down my back and I slid on my favorite Yeezy Boosts Brayden had scored for me. Outfit complete—I actually looked like I belonged in this city, even thought I still felt discombobulated. I had emotions going on that I didn't know what to do with, no convenient box to stuff them into.

I had a strong feeling Lucas would bear the brunt of them. I also had a feeling he would deal with it just fine, and I wasn't sure if that scared me more or less than anything.

As promised, Lucas was walking through the lobby when I came off the elevator. As soon as I saw him, that hard yank of attraction between us hadn't dulled but in fact had gotten sharper. As I balanced on the edge of that blade, the heat of the danger raced through me.

We'd stopped inches from each other and stared. It'd been weeks since I'd seen him but somehow it felt longer, and I felt disconnected, despite our conversation last night.

"I was coming up to get you," he said finally.

"I know—but I need to eat." And really, I couldn't have fully blamed him for what would've happened if he'd shown at my door. I wanted to kiss him right now and take him back upstairs— the attraction crackled between us like static electricity. It was almost painful.

"Come on." He motioned but didn't touch me, like he knew that wouldn't get us out the door any faster, or at all. I followed him, the rumbling hunger in my stomach warring with the stirring between my legs.

I can have both, I reasoned. *Just not at the same time.*

Instead of climbing into a car, we walked along the city blocks. The night was perfect, crisp with the promise of more warmth to come tomorrow. And then Lucas casually put a hand on my lower back and steered me into a restaurant that appeared to be closed. And I supposed it was, to the general public.

There were about ten people there already. "So they're still open?"

"No, this is a private dinner for the chef and some friends." Lucas explained. "Usually, chefs will have their late night meals with other chefs."

"That makes sense. I can't imagine they'd have a lot of time to eat during the dinner rush," I said as one of the men broke from the group and came toward us, calling out, "Lucas—long time no see."

Lucas shook his hand, but then the man pulled him in for a hug. "Ryn, this is Mario. He's the owner and chef."

Mario shook my hand. "Welcome. Plenty of food."

"Thanks," I managed as the others from the group nodded in my direction. I recognized one of them as the man who'd been standing in the doorway of the gallery that first morning I'd met Lucas. He was dark-haired. Handsome in a very rough-strewn way. He looked like trouble all around and the scar that ran just off-center down the front of his neck was there as if to prove it true to those who didn't normally trust their instincts.

Still, he nodded in my direction but his eyes immediately shot questions toward Lucas. Lucas ignored them in favor of looking at me and saying, "You're not in the mood for people. Or maybe I'm not."

I didn't argue. Two antisocial, hungry people getting cooked a private meal was a perfect way to put the day's happenings behind me.

But with him right across the table, somehow the distance was multiplying.

How I'd felt so close to him when he was miles away and yet so distant now when he was actually touching me was something I struggled with… until I realized that this was the way he wanted it. "So, that guy with the dark hair and the blue shirt—"

"Grant."

"Is he your bodyguard?"

Lucas snorted. "We'll go with that. He'll love

hearing that." It made me feel stupid and that must've shown on my face because Lucas was quick to add, "He's a good guy."

"Dangerous," I murmured.

"That too."

"Where were you?" I asked finally.

"Work."

"As? A traveling salesman? Because I can't picture you going door to door with encyclopedias, but unless you've got family money, you've got to do something to fund your apartment." I wanted to shut up, but I couldn't.

He sat back, looking resigned, like he'd expected this. "Security. With Grant. We're partners."

I hesitated. "You mean like…alarms?"

"We provide security measures for large companies." He poured me more wine while I let that sink in. "What else is on your mind?"

He was very in tune with me. I didn't think I liked it. "I just…you didn't commission me to paint for you, did you?"

"No."

"Would you tell me?"

He glanced up at me as he ate and nodded, and I didn't believe him, although not necessarily about the commissioned painting.

I pushed away, no longer interested in food or conversation. Paranoia began to overtake me.

What if Lucas made Meghan buy the session?

What if this was all a set-up and Lucas was a part of my past? Why couldn't I shake that feeling...and why wouldn't I remember him? "I need to get out of here."

He stood. "Let's go."

But I was already beginning my walk out of the restaurant, telling him, "I can get myself home."

He caught up to me fast. "I'm sure you can, but I'm not letting that happen," he said firmly. I didn't argue. The sooner I could get away from him and think clearly, the better. I'd been picking at him through dinner and I was pissed at myself and him. And I still wanted him, even though I pulled away physically as he attempted to tug me closer. "What the hell, Ryn? Come on, we had a good talk last night, didn't we?"

"So what? I should trust you implicitly now?"

"Enough to tell me what the fuck's going on in your head right now, yeah." He looked angry and confused. Pretty much exactly how I felt.

"Like you don't know," I shot back.

"I don't, so why don't you fucking tell me," he ground out. His face was a dark thunderstorm, a glower that made me take a step back...even though I somehow knew the anger wasn't directed at me.

Still, I didn't notice them, not until it was too

late, but Lucas had. Looking back, I realized his body language had him fighting on two fronts for several minutes before he turned to the purely physical.

There were three of them, none of them as tall as Lucas but they were broad, muscle-bound and although they didn't show any weapons, they acted like they carried them. Lucas stood in front of me and one of the men smiled.

"Cute, protecting her. Give us your cash and we'll think about letting you have sloppy seconds."

I realized we were partially hidden down an alley, and that it was very dark and deserted. I could scream, but Lucas was so still and I wanted to follow his lead.

I also wanted to control my temper, which started to flare as another man made suggestive motions with his hands and tongue, pointing at me. Lucas nodded, reached into his back pocket with one hand as if about to concede and hand over his wallet, but instead of grabbing his cash, the hand pushed me back into the corner as he went forward at them.

I'm prickly with sensation as goose bumps rise on my skin. Blood rushes, pounding a beat between my ears until it's all I hear. The scene in front of me plays out, wordless. Soundless. Silent slow motion.

And there's nothing but a palpable danger vibrating through me. My skin crawls, throat tightens. I've backed up to the bricks which scrape along my jacket, almost catching me to the surface.

It's like I'm watching something with another layer over it, an overexposed negative of one thing superimposed over another.

In front of me, Lucas is fighting three men.

But in my overexposed memory, I'm fighting someone—*something* else, even though Lucas isn't letting any of these men near me.

A sob racks through me but I stifle it. I need to be strong.

Activity resumes at its normal volume. The gauzy curtain lifts to reveal real life and I see and hear the fight happening inches from me. The sounds of bodies scraping against concrete and fists making contact with flesh and bone overwhelm my already fragile senses.

I look down and realize that, at some point, I've pulled the knife out of my bag to protect myself in case they came near me, but Lucas was fighting like he could take all of them.

And he could. Because he did. There were curses. Bottles breaking. Blood. A violent, impressive blur that left one man limping away from the scene as fast as he could and the other two on the ground. Lucas took one of their wallets in hand, pocketed the man's ID, making sure both of them saw what he was doing.

And still, I'm ready to fight. I'm dizzy. Sweating. My brain is a jumbled mess of chaotic images flashing in front of me like a slideshow and I'm desperately trying to pick it all apart.

One man groaned and one didn't move. Lucas kicked the groaning one, then bent down and whispered something in his ear. Then he took the knife from my hand, folded it and put it away, all without seeming surprised at my having it.

Only then did he turn to me and say, "Let's go."

I'm safe. He's saved me again, the heat from his body reassuring in its proximity. And then he walked me away. As we walked quickly, I heard sirens. We went down a couple of alleys and made it to the next cross street, far enough away to not be noticed. Lucas didn't look very much like he'd been in a fight and the way we were wrapped around each other made it appear we were just another couple out late and enjoying each other's company.

I couldn't help but be impressed by Lucas's dead calm show of temper, his silent, impressive fury. The violence didn't bother me, but it had triggered me as always. Sometimes it brought me back to the past event that I remembered and sometimes it flashed ever so briefly to one I couldn't quite pull into focus. Still, it had me trembling with leftover adrenaline that raced through me, even though I hadn't been the one to fight.

We got back to my apartment quickly, and without talking. He ushered me inside and I turned off the alarm and immediately went to get ice. He was flexing his hand, which was cut and slightly swollen, but apart from that and a light bruise on his cheek, he was none the worse for wear.

He put his hand down on the counter and I put the towel-wrapped ice on the top of his hand gently.

I was shaking slightly.

And I wanted to take all my clothes off. And his. "I'm not sure I've ever been more turned on in my life," I admitted.

He nodded, his eyes hooded. "Fucking and fighting aren't far apart at all. Some say it's all the same emotion."

I'd never connected the two, but the way my heart was beating, adrenaline racing through my blood, like my nervous system was on an all-out assault…

No, the two weren't far apart at all. "One's more satisfying."

One side of his mouth lifted in a slight grin. "You've never really fought to win, then." He poured a glass of scotch I assumed was for him but he pushed it at me. I downed it quickly, enjoying the burn. "I'm sorry, Ryn."

"For what? For saving me from a bunch of thugs?" I handed him the glass, waited until he put it down before pulling him down to me and kissing him, split lip be damned. I tasted the metallic tang of blood, let my mouth swallow his groan. I ground against him. "Why is it okay when you fight?"

"I don't know—it just is, okay?"

"It shouldn't be," I insisted.

"I'll keep that in mind next time three guys try to jump us. I'll let you save me."

"Fuck you."

"That's how I was hoping the night would go." He pulled back from me reluctantly and I let him. My body needed him, but we'd somehow become strangers. We *were* strangers. Something triggered in me and I didn't know how to handle it. And it wasn't like I could explain it to him, but somehow, he sensed it. All of it.

"What the fuck's going on with you? You started to tell me before we were interrupted."

"I painted Meghan today," I blurted out, because it was suddenly obvious that he didn't know anything about it. "A nude." He stared at me like I was from another planet. "She bought me—a portrait session at an auction. Brayden made me do it to rehab my image."

"Brayden thought painting Meghan nude would rehab your image?"

"He didn't think that far ahead."

"He doesn't know Meghan the way I do," he muttered, then tilted his head and looked at me. "You knew you had to paint her last night, when we talked."

Right. Um… "Yes."

"Yes?" His brows raised. "You know I could've put a stop to it then, right?"

"And made me look like a jerk to the charity committee. You know there was no way out. You weren't even in the city."

"There's always a way out," he growled. "I could've called in my bid. I would've bought the commission."

"And I would've painted you nude?" I attempted a joke, but he wasn't laughing, was dead serious when he said, "Yes. So now you owe me."

"I owe *you*?"

"Yes," he said calmly. "For several things—you said so yourself."

I had. "You left without calling."

He frowned slightly. "I won't do that again."

"Why did you?"

"You didn't seem like you wanted me to bother you. I knew you'd call if you needed me. That's the way you seemed to want it."

"But if I'd called you…" I trailed off. He didn't bother to answer—he didn't have to. He already had with his actions.

Dammit.

He took a step closer. "I'm who you see, Ryn. I'm a moody, goddamned pain in the ass who'd drop everything at a moment's notice for you. And you know that. Think I've let a lot of women toy with me that way?"

I shook my head.

"Good. Stop second-guessing me. Don't play games. I don't. If you need to talk, call me."

"You needed me the other night—"

"And I called," he reminded me. "I wanted to call a lot more, but I know your work's important to you."

"I don't know how to do this."

"I just told you how. Don't complicate it."

"Fine."

"Are we done talking?" he asked as he started to unbutton his shirt. "Because you owe me a painting."

"You really want me to paint you?"

"You said you wanted to," he reminded me, his shirt open to expose his chest. Big. Broad. Abs looked painted on. But he was also scarred, evidence of a difficult life lived, of secrets I had yet to know about. But I wanted to know.

Definitely.

I brushed my thumbs over his cheekbones, ran them over his jawline. *Brutally handsome.*

The urge to take him to bed immediately flooded my body at the same time the urge to paint kicked in. Stupid cockblocking muse.

The other night had been about slaking a need, for both of us. Tonight, I wanted to look. Stare. And Lucas was going to let me.

I chose painting. "Fine. Everything off."

"One condition."

"Backing out already, Lucas?"

"Never, sweetheart. But I think you should give as good as you get. I want you naked too."

I stared at him, trying to decide if he was really just crazy or what. "Why would I do that?"

"Gives me something to look at."

I was far from shy and he'd seen me naked anyway. Defiantly, I pushed the thin straps of my dress off my shoulder, one after the other unceremoniously. The dress puddled at my feet and I stepped out of it toward him. And I climbed him—he held me up with zero effort. I wrapped myself around him, naked to his fully clothed as the heat swelled and the idea of painting him faded into the background.

Things were good. But the violence of the fight was still unsettling me, reminding me of the danger all around me. "Lucas…how can this work?"

"Seems to be working fine already."

"People will talk."

"Let them."

But he knew as well as I did that a hint of favoritism could turn public opinion against me. This could be the kiss of death for my fledgling career.

A career you didn't want, I reminded myself. Because, as Brayden said, I'd always have the work. No one could take that pleasure from me, unless I let them.

Unless I delved into my past and the painting faded. "This has to wait…"

"Until after you paint."

"Until after I paint," I agreed.

"I can handle it if you can."

That was definitely a dare, and one I wasn't sure I'd win. But I'd be damned if I didn't try. I peeled off him and motioned for him to lie down as I said, "Make yourself comfortable."

"Not going to pose me?"

"I have a feeling it will be more interesting if you pose yourself."

He shrugged easily. "Have it your way." He made quick work of shrugging his shirt off his shoulders and stripping his pants. Naked, he grabbed a magazine and lay down on the couch in one fluid motion, comfortable as hell and unfazed by the attention. He had one arm folded under his head. The other was resting close to his cock, which was half hard and growing by the second. I bit my lip to keep focused, and let the sexual energy ramp up the drawing.

I had to force myself back to reality by grabbing for my supplies before I jumped onto the couch and back onto him.

I started off with charcoals, rolling the black sticks between my fingers to warm them—letting them smudge my fingers as I stared at him.

There were a few wrong starts. I ripped the paper off the pad viciously, because I knew what was wrong. I was too close. I was thinking about Lucas rather than letting the beast take over.

When I finally stopped being self-conscious, the sketch flowed, faster than I thought possible.

Suddenly, I'm thinking about the fight again, the danger, the way Lucas took care of those men like a warrior fighting to protect me. Instead of waning the way it often did after I'd finished working, the adrenaline surged through me like a driving need.

Lucas's eyes still held the same feral, dangerous hunger they had since the fight. I'd captured it in my sketch but it could never compare to the real-life version that currently stalked his way over to me.

And I wanted to be caught.

That driving need propelled me into his arms again, fully able to give myself over to this kind of satisfaction.

"You're goddamned beautiful, Ryn." His voice was a growl. "Watching you like that...a fucking gift."

He covered my mouth with his, and my arms wound around his shoulders. He lifted me like I weighed nothing, and I wrapped my legs around his waist. His arousal was hard against my belly, but Lucas wasn't in a rush. His mouth went to my neck and I arched against him as he scraped the sensitive flesh with his teeth.

No longer stretched between the need to create and the need for him, I could give myself wholly over to this. Moans of satisfaction I couldn't help escaped from the back of my throat.

It was mouths exploring, hands and fingers skimming as Lucas walked me over to the couch.

He laid me on it, his mouth taking my nipples and sucking hard as heat speared through me.

As he drove inside me, his mouth came down hungry on mine. A hand buried in my hair, keeping me close. Our need fed off each other's, making us both insatiable.

My skin was far too sensitive and the build of my orgasm was a powerful, surging rush. I convulsed, clamped around him as he pulled my hips tight against his.

Slick heat, absorbing the sensation of his orgasm, letting my sex stroke him dry. Watching him lose control because of me.

He rested his forehead against my shoulder. His skin was slick with sweat, binding us together.

I didn't want to release him. I kept my trembling legs wrapped around him by sheer will. And he was still hard inside me.

We lay, tangled, the cool fall air drifting over our naked bodies from an opened window in the kitchen. I shivered and he grabbed for the blanket we'd knocked to the ground, wrapping us up.

"When do I get to see my picture?"

"When it goes on sale," I said innocently. "You need to stand next to it, holding a sign that says,

'Objects appear larger than they truly are.'"

He rolled his eyes. "The smile on your face says otherwise."

"Because you know me so well."

His tone got serious then. "Yes, Ryn. I do."

"How can you be so sure about me—about us?"

"I've always followed my gut, same as you," Lucas pointed out. "For some reason, you're hiding from it."

Because I'm terrified of putting you in danger. But I couldn't bring myself to say that, and my throat felt tight and painful, making anything but a small shrug impossible.

His arms tightened around me. His warm breath grazed my ears, and then his teeth tugged my earlobe. I shivered, melted against him, my body showing me exactly where my instincts were, and all of them pushing me farther into Lucas's arms…and his world.

I never wanted to leave. "Keep me safe."

He pulled back and stared. "Try and stop me."

8

I DIDN'T REMEMBER FALLING asleep, hadn't wanted to lose any more precious time with Lucas, but I woke with him straining at the sheets next to me, writhing quietly in what appeared to be the throes of a nightmare.

I was far too familiar with it. Gingerly, I began to move away so he wouldn't flail against me. I wasn't worried about being hit but I figured he'd be upset if he did so, even unintentionally. And then I began to call to him in a low, soothing voice, attempting to bring him back to present day and company.

Finally, he started to pull himself out of it. When he opened his eyes and sat up with a start, I moved closer to him and murmured, "Hey, it's me. You're okay. You're awake now and everything's okay."

He blinked hard a few times and looked around.

"We're at my place," I added and after half a second he nodded, acknowledging me before muttering, "Shit. Sorry."

"That's okay. Happens to me all the time."

Immediately, he was far more alert than he'd been seconds before, his gaze focused on me. "You have a lot of nightmares?"

My alarm bells were ringing quietly but that didn't stop me from agreeing with a nod. Then I added, "Everyone in my life has nightmares. I thought they were normal."

"That's so fucking sad." Lucas ran a hand through his sweat-soaked hair, and then he laughed and I did too, because I realized how utterly ridiculous it sounded, truth or not.

And it was the truth. I got up from the bed and grabbed a washcloth. I wet it and cooled him down with it, starting with his face and moving to his neck and shoulders, and he let me, sitting stiffly and finally letting out a long sigh.

When I finished, he asked, "Brayden has a lot of nightmares?"

"Sometimes." I stared at him. "Do you?"

"I don't actually sleep a lot." Which translated to 'yes' in my mind. "Definitely not with a woman."

"I'm sure there's been a parade of them," I said

dryly.

He didn't try to deny it. "I have a past, Ryn. But you're my future."

"I like hearing that."

"Good. Get used to it."

I decided to push my luck. "Do I get to know about your past?" I left off the 'with women' part of the sentence, but Lucas wasn't stupid.

"What do you want to know?" His tone was unguarded but his body language wasn't.

"You've been in love."

"Yes," he said, almost cautiously. Of course, I'd wanted him to say no. "I mean, as much as I could've been."

"You were young?"

"Young enough to not know better," he admitted. "It was long distance."

"But you still remember her."

"I thought she was the one," he said quietly, and I was immediately, unrepentantly jealous.

"Where is she now?" I asked, hoping I was managing to keep the slight edge out of my voice.

"Far away."

"Is it bad that I'm relieved by that?"

"It's not something I want you to worry about," he told me.

"But you loved her."

He smiled. "I didn't know her, but I wanted to."

"You connected. I understand." I pointed to my *Man in Trees* portraits. "That's what those are about."

His eyes had a faraway look in them when he said, "Someone you wanted to love."

I nodded, stopping just short of saying, 'Someone I do.' But I was staring at him, saying that with my eyes about both the man in the pictures and him. Out loud, I simply said, "Yes," then melted against him.

"I guess we've both been through it," he murmured.

"Seems that way." He knew nothing, really, about my past, no more than the rest of the world did. But I think he knew there was more to the story. It wouldn't interest him, not with the same morbid, tabloid-like curiosity it would the rest of the world. He'd want to know how best to protect me.

The best way to protect him was to keep him away from me. God, how fucked up this all was… and how amazing at the same time.

LATE THE NEXT AFTERNOON, I was paging through a few magazines Brayden had brought in with my mail when I came across an article I'd been dreading…and it wasn't even about me.

I slid it over toward Brayden. "I guess he's headed to the big leagues."

Brayden's gaze slid over the picture of my ex and ignored the carefully constructed article that I'm sure didn't talk about Jared Connor's complete and utter disdain for anyone's talent but his own.

But maybe that was just a bitter ex talking.

"His new book's coming out this week. There's lots of buzz around it because everything's under wraps. It's already been optioned for a movie."

I nodded. Jared had already found good, steady commercial success with his fiction, but, as Brayden and I had discussed, Jared was one of those people who would never be satisfied with his success, no matter how big. He would chase it relentlessly.

"I'm sure it's inevitable I'll run into him," I said.

"Maybe sooner than you think," Brayden murmured, then handed me an invite. Thick-papered and important-looking.

To Jared's book launch party.

"He invited me?"

"There's a handwritten note," he told me. "I was trying to decide if I should give it to you or burn it. But this shit…" He pointed to the magazine. "Synchronicity at its best."

Reluctantly, I pulled the creamy cardstock all the way out of the envelope and saw Jared's writing, elegant and practiced as always.

Ryn, I'd love to see you there.

-J

Such a comfortable note, as though we'd ended on good terms. Knowing his level of interpretational skills, he probably thought we did. I glanced up at Brayden. "Talk to me."

"I'd never make you go to this."

"But?"

He sighed. "It's a huge event. Good coverage. Good, trendy and diverse crowd who buys and commissions art, and who'd be interested in a crazy artist who starts fights at her own shows and dates Lucas Caine."

"Christ." I rubbed my temples and protested, "I thought I was rehabilitated."

Brayden snorted. "It'd be helpful to get the haute and hot set on your side. Or some of them, at least."

Maybe seeing Jared at a big party was the best way. We were both successful. I was over him, moved on. It was time to break the ice. "When is it?"

"Tomorrow night."

"So I'm a last-minute invite."

"All invites went out last minute to maintain the integrity of the project," Brayden read from the invite. "This was hand-delivered to the doorman."

"Fine," I said through gritted teeth.

"I can't go with you though," Brayden said.

"Bray!"

"I figured you'd want Lucas."

"I don't know if we're doing that," I said truthfully.

He shrugged. "As good a time as any to find out."

I was stressed at the thought of the book party, so much so that I threw myself into my work and didn't come out until the following morning. I slept for a while and then I decided I needed to run to get rid of the excess nervous energy.

I still hadn't heard from Lucas. Hadn't called him either. Because what if he couldn't go with me tonight?

What if you'd just asked him yesterday as soon as Brayden told you?

Because I was the queen of procrastination, dammit. And I needed some time to be alone, to process the fact that I'd be seeing the one man I'd thought I loved so much that I revealed my past—or lack of—to.

Stupid, stupid, stupid.

I dressed and put my headphones on, plugged my iPod in. Rap and classic rock alternately blasted through the Beats as my feet hit the pavement first on the way to the park, and then the soft dirt of the trails, in rhythm to the songs.

I sang the lyrics in my head as the pleasant burn in my muscles kicked in. I left everything behind—everything and everyone—letting it fall away from my shoulders. I started singing silently along with the lyrics. No one would give me a second glance in New York doing this. Everyone seemed to be talking to themselves.

But after a time I became aware of an echo on the ground, another heavy set of feet running behind me. I turned down my music and yes, I heard the footsteps.

But Central Park, mid-afternoon, jogging… *hello*.

And still, something in my gut didn't sit right. Not at all. I kept my pace as I ran up, right behind a group of women. Safety in numbers.

When they stopped, I stopped. Looked around under the pretense of stretching and saw nothing beyond other joggers, walkers. Moms with strollers. People rollerblading. And unless they were together, no one was giving anyone a second look.

Alone in a crowd.

I wasn't usually paranoid. Not like this. Maybe the thought of the party was making me crazy, but I couldn't deny that my skin crawled. I fought off the panic attack as I walked briskly out of the park and into the crowded streets.

Nothing can happen to you here for sure. Look at all the people.

People dropped out of sight in broad daylight every day. I knew that was true.

I started to jog again. I didn't look over my shoulder. Suppose I saw someone I wasn't supposed to...

Suppose I turned around to find my past, hot on my heels? The thought was the nail in the coffin. My panic washed over me like a wave and I stumbled under the powerful weight of the tide.

My chest was tight.

My lungs hurt.

My breath rasps. I'm frantic.

Someone's getting closer, and I'm screaming. But the screams are only in my mind, and they echo my panic, my deepest, darkest fears, deafening me internally.

This kind of fear makes me hysterical. For several minutes, it threatens to freeze me, render me limp. Useless.

Prey.

But I'm stronger than that. Sharks smell blood in the water. I won't let myself be a victim. Not when there's breath left in me.

I was so thankful than Brayden had helped me to map out the closest police stations to where I liked to run—I also made sure I knew how to get there without my phone but it seemed silly to stop and call the police.

I didn't want to stop running.

When I got to the front steps of the police

station, I mingled with a few police in uniform walking up the steps. I tried to remain calm but I wasn't succeeding because one of them said, "Ma'am, do you need some help?" and I looked over my shoulder, saw no one and nodded.

A few minutes later, I was parked next to an officer's desk, paper towels and water in hand, followed by some orange juice. They'd also given me a police department sweatshirt to wear, because I'd started to shiver from my post-run cool down.

"So someone's broken into your apartment twice, but you didn't report it." The police officer named Lenny Burns repeated my story a few minutes later, making it—and me—sound incredibly stupid. "And then someone followed you today in the park. Was anything taken from your apartment?"

"Not exactly. No. I mean, something was left. Flowers."

"Flowers," he repeated. "Both times?"

"Yes. They were placed in my apartment. I didn't put them there and my friend is the only other one with a key."

"And he definitely didn't put them there?"

I *didn't ask him...* "No, he didn't."

"Any idea who could've done that? Do you have enemies?"

I stared at him. "Yes…no." God, this was a mistake.

"Do you have the flowers?"

"No. One set disappeared and I threw the others out."

The officer didn't blink, just sat back and put his pen down deliberately when I said *disappeared*.

I sounded crazy. "It's true," I insisted.

"I can't do anything without evidence."

"I just want to know what my options are."

"Sweetheart, this isn't a takeout menu, it's the police station. People come here to report real crimes, not just discuss their options." He sat back. "I'm going to be frank with you. I'm not sure if you're really believing this or if you're purposely wasting my time."

"I'm not. I'm just scared."

His expression softened. "I see that. Maybe you should talk to someone about all this…"

He thinks I'm crazy. And I couldn't totally deny that. I sometimes joked with Brayden that he should watch out for me, that I could be an escaped mental patient. "I'm sorry. I know how this sounds."

"There are restraining orders, but you have to know who's stalking you. Look, if you spot the person, or if there's a history, you can tell me."

No, I couldn't. "Thanks for your help."

"Is there someone you can call to pick you up?"

The implication was clear—*You're a fragile flower who'll melt down at shadows in the street and then you'll come in again.*

I pulled my phone out and dialed Lucas.

He picked up on the first ring. "What's wrong?"

"I'm at the police station. Can you come get me?"

He didn't ask anything beyond, "Are you hurt?" and when I told him I wasn't he said, "Give me ten."

And ten minutes later, he was there, his hand on my shoulder but addressing Lenny Burns. "What happened?"

The officer stood. "She says she was followed."

Lucas's eyes narrowed and the officer realized he'd made a mistake in thinking he had an ally. "You don't believe her? She says she's being followed, then she's being followed."

"Why not call the police when her apartment got broken into?"

"Because of the same dismissive treatment she's just received, I'd imagine," Lucas said.

"I realize Ms. Taylor's gained some notoriety over the past weeks, but she's going to have to hire private security to deal with the kinds of issues she's describing. They'll be able to collect the evidence she's saying she was, ah, *unable* to save."

Lucas remained stone-faced, which made the officer shift after several moments. Only after that did Lucas tell him, "Thanks. I'll take it from here."

Lucas drove us back to my apartment, pulled up front and gave his keys to my doorman. I'd been quiet on the ride, unable to wrap my mind around all of it and now, Lucas put his arm around me reassuringly. He was strong. I knew that. Strong enough to handle me and my past…but would he want to?

"Thanks for the rescue," I managed as I tried to get my key into the lock on my apartment door. Lucas took it from me and got us inside in seconds. "Again."

"You're shaken up. Don't be so hard on yourself."

"I guess I should've been working out with you at three in the morning instead."

He frowned. "I don't want to take away your freedom of doing things alone, Ryn."

The 'but' was implied. But, it would happen. It wasn't safe for me to be alone and it seemed like Lucas believed that. Believed *me*. "I didn't tell Brayden about the flowers either."

"Why not?"

"I didn't want to worry him. I figured there must be an explanation. And…" I drew in a deep breath. "I do have panic attacks. I haven't taken meds for them in a while, so sometimes I can overreact. But I didn't dream the flowers. Or the person following me."

Lucas just nodded.

"Do you think it has anything to do with those guys from the other night?" I asked now.

"Definitely not. They're taken care of."

I wasn't sure I wanted to know exactly what that meant but I chose to believe him. "Okay, so…"

"I'll get you a treadmill. I'll run with you outside. I'll set up cameras in your apartment. But…" That damned word again. "You have to tell Brayden this. I won't let you keep stuff from someone who's got your back."

That was true. More than anyone, Brayden would support me through thick and thin. "Deal."

I grabbed my phone and prepared to text Brayden when I saw his most recent text. Reminding my about Jared's book party. That was tonight.

I didn't want to go. God, I'd rather do anything else. But the odd timing of the invite and the tightness in my throat…something urged me to go.

Shit.

Maybe it was nothing. But these days, whenever I had this feeling, it never was. "I have to go to a book party tonight," I blurted out.

"Didn't realize that was required."

I was too worried to joke back. "It's an ex." A frown crossed his face. "Years ago. Short relationship."

"Okay," he said slowly.

"I don't know why, but I have to go," I blurted out. His gaze narrowed, and then he nodded. Lucas lived by his gut—he would always understand a confession like the one I'd just given him.

"I'll be with you."

"So we're doing this?"

Lucas frowned. "What's this?"

"Going places together."

"Yes."

"Okay then." I took a deep breath. "Thanks. Hopefully, it'll be nothing," I tacked on quickly.

He didn't rush in to reassure me.

While I slept, Grant had dropped off clothes for Lucas. I found them draped over my couch and heard the shower running when I woke.

I entertained joining him in the shower, but

before I could make a move, there was a knock on my door. I figured it must be Brayden, since no one buzzed me from downstairs. But when I opened the door, I cursed myself for not checking first. Because it was Dan Turner. "How'd you get up here?"

"The doorman knows me," he said with a shrug. "We talked about how you had a scare today."

"Do you think it was the person who stole my painting?" I asked irritably, in no mood to play nice.

"Good comeback. It doesn't change the fact that you're in trouble."

I narrowed my eyes. "How do you know that, when the officer who took my statement didn't even believe me?"

"Like I told you the first time we met, you're hanging out with questionable people," he retorted.

"And Brayden and Lucas are following me now to scare me?"

Dan Turner shook his head. "You just don't get it. *You're* under investigation."

"By the police?"

"By the insurance company I represent. Eventually, the case will get turned over to the police."

"I haven't done anything wrong."

"We'll see about that. And I'm not sure you can say the same about your friends. Lucas is a violent, dangerous man. He's unpredictable."

"Obviously, I'm a good match, seeing as I've been called violent and unpredictable myself in several recent articles," I told him evenly. "Now get the fuck out of my hallway."

As my voice rose on those last words, Lucas came barreling out of the bathroom, obviously fresh from the shower, still dripping, a towel barely hanging around his waist. I moved aside, since it was obvious who his target was. He stopped mere inches from Turner, who had the nerve to smile.

I wouldn't have, not the way Lucas's eyes glittered. Then again, the way Lucas was acting proved Turner's point about the danger. Granted, it was nothing I hadn't known about or accepted.

"Don't come near her again," Lucas warned Turner, his voice a dangerous growl that took my breath away.

"You're really going to put yourself in this position? Again?" Turner's laugh was nasty and sent a different kind of chill down my spine than Lucas's voice had.

I wanted to pull Lucas away, to protect him, which seemed ridiculous. But the need was so urgent I found myself tugging on his arm, trying to get between him and Turner.

"To protect Ryn? Damned right, Turner. Step off."

"Just to be clear—that's a threat, correct?"

"It's a truth." Lucas tore his gaze away from Turner's to meet mine, since I hadn't stopped pulling on his arm. Immediately, his expression softened and he let me lead him away from Turner, who slowly backed himself out of my doorway.

Lucas closed the door purposefully in his face and locked it.

"I'm losing track of all the times you've saved me at this point."

I swore I heard the smile in his voice when he said, "Is that how it's supposed to work—me saving you?"

"I don't know how it's supposed to work," I said honestly.

"No one's ever defended you?"

"Not like this."

"Get used to it," he growled, and then he bent his head and kissed me deeply. He was going to prove his words to me, whether I liked it or not. As his tongue stroked mine, his hands slid along my hips, holding them tight, rocking me against his hardness.

His arms tightened around me, holding me. Protecting me.

Claiming me, once again, but this time it was

different. It felt different. Before, sex had been all about slaking an incredible thirst. There was still a frenzied quality between us—Lucas had somehow gotten into my bloodstream and ramped me up like no one before him.

But tonight, it was all completely different. Next level, admitting that this was far more than a series of one-night stands.

Vulnerability was an emotion I didn't wear well. Around Lucas, I seemed to let the walls down far too easily. I wasn't sure if that said more about me or him, but he'd come for me today, without hesitation.

He'd stood up for me.

He believed me.

What more was there?

I pulled away from him and he stared at me. And then he smiled when I did a semi-dance with him, turning him so his back was against the wall.

When I sank to my knees and unwrapped his towel, he groaned. When I freed his cock and rubbed the broad head with my finger first, I looked up to see him put his head back against the wall, baring his throat, as it were.

Allowing me. King of the jungle, letting me in. Letting me take him, taste him. And I did, swallowing him first and feeling his utter control as he tried not to jut his hips. I loved this feeling of control. It had been taken from me, in the park, by the police, but never from Lucas.

I could feel the strength in his thighs, the tension in his muscles as I suckled the sensitive bundle of nerves along the underside of his cock. I loved hearing him hiss above me. I was wet, could probably come just from doing this to him. And he was close too, but he stopped me with his hands on my head, gently urging me up off my knees.

"You taste good," I murmured against his ear and his groan rumbled against my chest, deep and powerful and utterly, completely for me.

"You fucking undo me, Ryn."

"Trouble," I reminded him.

"Trouble," he agreed as we moved together into the bathroom, our bodies still together. He reached in to start the shower and he kissed me again, and as he did so, he was also stripping me.

It was a perfect metaphor, since that's what he'd been doing to me since we'd first met at the gallery—he'd been stripping me of fearing him, of worrying about one-night stands and his reputation.

Finally, my clothes were on the ground. We swayed together, skin to skin in the now steaming room, me with Lucas.

Nothing had changed—from the second I'd

met him, I'd known he was a man of actions to back up his words.

Everything had changed. Between us, there was an understanding. I'd never thought anything could happen this fast. I was too careful. To untrusting.

"You're safe with me," he told me, like he could read my expression. To be fair, I wasn't trying to hide the emotion. It was too big, welling up and threatening to expose everything I'd never wanted exposed.

But I stopped just short of that and in response, he picked me up. My legs wrapped around him. I was in post-work-out sweat and grunge and it didn't matter. His skin smelled male and perfect and I bit his shoulder as he carried me into the shower.

The warmth of the water hit my skin, and we stood under the spray, kissing until we couldn't breathe. And then we kissed more, straining against each other, wanting to make all of this last.

10

WE FINALLY ARRIVED AT Jared's party, Lucas with damp hair, me flushed and looking so obviously (and recently) post sex that we might as well have worn a sign. Lucas could get away with going anywhere half naked. In his jeans and black sweater and boots, he looked perfect. I, however, needed work, but thankfully, the party was dark and moody with its low lighting and crowded space. In this high-rise penthouse, people mingled, artists, writers and the wealthy socialites who funded us.

"Do you know a lot of these people?" He nodded but didn't look thrilled about it. "And they know you?" Now he stared at me like I had several heads. "I just...maybe you know them like a fan does?"

"A fan?" he asked slowly, like the word was

foreign to him. "Are you going to be embarrassing in here?"

"Me? No. I mean, I don't think so."

"Christ," he muttered and held my hand as we snaked through the crowd. He snagged me a glass of champagne and I took a couple of fast sips, aware that I hadn't eaten since morning. I wanted to be relaxed, not make a drunken fool of myself. I managed to flag down a waiter with a tray of appetizers—tiny cheese quiches—and when I turned back around, having taken my hand from Lucas's, I found him talking to a tall, dark-haired woman. She had a heavy accent, French, and she touched Lucas a bit too much for my tastes.

And of course, I spotted Meghan across the room.

"This is the most incestuous bunch of people," I muttered. And heard a laugh from next to me. "Shit."

"Don't worry—I have weirdly exceptional hearing, and I feel the same way."

She was shorter than me. Very pretty, tanned, confident. And… "Wait, you're on TV."

She smiled. "I'm Gabrielle."

Gabrielle Weston. She was a TV star. She was really hot right now, according to the magazines Brayden had lying around. "I'm Ryn."

"Oh, the artist. Brayden's friend." She grabbed

my hand and smiled even more warmly. "I've got your *Color Study* in my living room."

"Oh, wow. Cool." I never knew what I was supposed to say to that, but she said, "My manager dragged me here because the book's movie rights have been optioned." She shrugged. "I'm considering this an open audition since Jared has a say in the casting, which is really unusual."

It was, but it made sense to me. It definitely wasn't the norm for the author of the book-turned-movie to have much of a say in the film— that's what Jared had told me. But Jared's family was wealthy, and in the film industry. Jared had always been working on screenplays as well as novels, and he'd sold a short-lived sitcom at one point. It wouldn't surprise me if it was his family's pull that allowed Jared to have more of a role than he probably should have.

I made some more small talk with her, until her manager came up and introduced himself, then said, "Gabby, Jared wants to meet you."

She handed me her card. "Call me for lunch so we can talk art, okay?"

Before I could promise anything, I turned to see Jared walking to meet Gabriella halfway. I turned and tried to be invisible, not ready to see him just yet. I heard Jared's voice, the slow, southern drawl, and humiliation flashed through me.

God, I thought I was past that. I edged into the crowd until Lucas's hand closed around my elbow.

"Where are you going?"

"Hungry," I lied. "I also need some air. It's too much in here."

Lucas knew what I meant. He pointed to a doorway. "There's an open foyer through there. Go hang out for a few—I'll hunt down some food for you but there's a line. Call me if you need me sooner than later."

I didn't wait—I headed toward the open space and breathed deeply once I got there. It was quiet and private. A haven in the middle of the claustrophobia of the party happening on the other side of the wall. The door that led to the hallway of the building was open for better airflow and I could see out to the back set of elevators.

I leaned against a bookshelf by the opened door and closed my eyes.

When I opened them, I wasn't alone. Jared was there. "I thought I saw you earlier." He moved toward me, murmuring, "Fuck, I hate these things. I drank too much and I thought I was seeing things…"

And I thought *I* was the dramatic one. "You invited me, remember?"

"Right, yes. But I didn't know if you'd come."

"I RSVP'd," I said, but we both knew that didn't

guarantee anything. It was kind of nice to see him admitting how unsure he was about me coming, how badly he seemed to want me there. "I didn't know your publisher would throw you such a big party."

He gave a small smile. "Way to massage my ego."

"I didn't think it needed to get any bigger."

"Ouch," he said, hand over his heart. "I guess I deserved that."

He did. The way I remembered it, at that time I'd massaged it way too much, until I'd realized I was part of a stable of women for him, all eager to heap praise on his latest manuscript.

He laughed. "God, Ryn, you always made me laugh. I'm such a moody fuck and you didn't let me get away with it."

He ran a hand through his short, dark hair. He was too close—literally. Too close to my truth. He was the kind of guy you ended up admitting too much to. He was like an archeologist, always digging, sifting through conversations, using what he discovered and capturing it in his books.

His book. This latest one was poised be an immediate, huge commercial success. There'd be a movie. International attention.

He'd already had some literary success but now, with this commercial success, he would become the sell-out he'd said he'd never wanted to be. But before I could remind him of this, a woman with a pinched face and severely pulled-back hair stuck her head in the doorway and said, "Jared, it's time for your speech."

She left without acknowledging my presence after he nodded at her. Then he told me, "That's my agent. She keeps me on track."

"She looks like a bitch."

"She was, until I made her money."

"Go ahead, they're waiting. It was really good to see you."

"Ryn, please." He took a step in my direction and his hand wound around my wrist gently. "Stay. I'd like you to hear me speak."

Thankfully he let go of me and moved away just as fast as he'd come in. My pulse raced, fight or flight, as though he was bringing me danger rather than asking me to listen to a speech.

Don't ignore your gut, Ryn.

I moved out of the quiet space and just enough into the crowd to hear the rustle of excitement beginning to spread about the impending announcement.

The contents and cover of Jared's newest book had been kept secret.

Gabrielle ended up in front of me. I tugged on her sleeve and she turned and smiled.

"How did the meeting go?" I asked.

"Really well. Like, really well."

"You sound like you got the part."

She shrugged modestly. "Nothing's official yet, but he did share the premise with me. And I've got a copy of the script." A woman began introducing Jared into a microphone, causing the room to quiet down considerably. "I'd share spoilers with you, but you're about to find out about as much as I know."

Jared got up in front of the crowd, looking very comfortable there. "I want to thank you all for your interest in my newest book, *Over My Shoulder*. The book is ready for release tonight at midnight, and you'll all leave here with copies. The movie script has also been finished for some time. We've begun the process of casting and I've actually given out some scripts tonight to prospective actors, so I'm really thrilled. This book—the first in what will be a trilogy—really pushed my boundaries, and will push yours as well. It's a dark, psychological thriller, and I know it's my best work to date."

I sighed mentally and wished I was anywhere but here. Once the speech was over, I was so out of here.

"The premise of this book is a woman with amnesia," Jared explained, and a strange buzz started between my ears. "Our narrator can't remember anything before the age of seventeen. She's an author—a relentless author, I'd call her. She can't help but write. She gets famous with the help of a benefactor, but her past comes back to haunt her, and our hero helps to heal her, so to speak, by discovering where she really came from."

A soft "ohhh" went rippling through the crowd at the same time a chill went down my spine. I managed to breathe.

"It sounds fascinating," Gabrielle whispered. "I can't wait to read it. I had to sign a nondisclosure about the script but I'm sure it's going to mirror the book closely." I was frozen. There was no way Gabrielle could miss it, and she frowned. "Ryn, come, you're pale as hell. You need to sit."

No, I shouldn't have come here. "I need to sit," I echoed. "I'll be okay. You stay. Mingle," I told her, my voice surprisingly steady as I made my way back toward the empty space where I'd first talked to Jared tonight. Except I moved farther, through the room and headed toward the doorway to lead me to the hallway with the elevator.

I'd become fodder for his book.

His goddamned book was about a man who wants to help a woman find her lost past. Enough would be changed to protect me…for now. But I knew.

"Is the heroine, Kaia, based on a real-life person?" one of the reporters was asking, and it was enough to make me halt my march out of the apartment. Another reporter called out, "An ex-girlfriend, maybe?"

The audience laughed, but not loudly. They were all intent on hearing Jared's answer, which came after a momentary pause.

"Authors are always asked where we get our ideas, or whether we base our characters on real people. The answers are everywhere and yes, in that order, but that doesn't mean Kaia is based on any single person. There are parts of me in that character—in all my characters. And they always say, write what you know."

It was a good answer, but no one believed him. No one wanted to believe him.

"It's definitely based on a real-life person," I heard someone say.

"So, what do you think?" I heard Jared ask next and I turned, because he was asking me.

"You're kidding me, right?" I hissed at him. I had my arms drawn tightly against myself but I unwound them when I saw he was holding two glasses, and extending one in my direction. At least the asshole had the decency to realize this would be a blow to me, but not enough decency not to write the damned book in the first place.

"What the hell, Jared?"

He sighed. "Look, I never planned this. Not when you first told me," he said, his voice quiet. "But then I saw your paintings at Brayden's gallery—a few years ago—and I started thinking about the story you'd told me. Frankly, I always thought you made it up. But it didn't matter because I was going to change it."

"But you didn't."

"Some of the details are changed—it's not a memoir. It's labeled fiction. I made up a past for you," he said helpfully.

"How awesome of you, really," I said, my voice dripping sarcasm and hatred at once. "You're so thoughtful. Makes me all warm and fuzzy inside. You asshole. And I can't believe you planned the release around my show."

"Well, just in case." At least he had the decency to look sheepish about that. It still made me want to punch him, especially when he added, "You'd get a shitload of free publicity if we did link our careers."

He didn't get that there might be a lot of danger involved. That's how wrapped up in himself he was.

I didn't know if Gabrielle, or whatever actress got the role of me, would be in danger as well. I'd think anyone playing me would be. Then again,

I didn't know anything and Jared's made-up past was just that.

I flashed back to that Sunday afternoon, the day after I'd exposed what I knew about my past to Jared…and as he dropped me back at my Catskills apartment he decided that he couldn't be "tied down."

I knew it was partially the truth but I still hated him for saying it, probably because he wasn't the right man to help me leave my past behind. I'd wanted to seem more worldly, like of course I didn't want a relationship either, but I couldn't pull it off fully. It had been like a knife through the gut.

We'd been dating for six months up until that point. He'd been living in the city and commuting up to the Catskills because the quiet was necessary for his muse—his words, not mine. But on that particular weekend, he'd taken me away, farther upstate to a romantic inn, and that's when I decided I'd spill my guts about my past.

I'd thought it would make us closer. That it would change things. I'd wanted to show that I needed him, because he'd always said, "You don't need me the way I need you."

Which was, of course, a lie on both ends.

And when I'd stood there, stunned at his words, he'd reassured me with, "Ryn, it's okay.

You're young. We need to explore ourselves, spend time with other people. You'll thank me one day." But he'd also smirked a little as he said that, and it made him look more handsome. His face was sculptured planes. His lips were perfect. I'd fought the urge to close my eyes and trace them with my fingertips.

I realized I'd done that zone-out thing, and that he didn't seem to mind. He didn't find it cutely amusing or stupidly spacey like most. "You don't belong here. You have talent, Ryn."

"Thank you," I'd managed. "But I like it here. It's nice."

"You won't grow with nice."

I'd gotten angry then, at both myself and him. "Maybe I'm happy the way I am."

"Maybe you're lying to yourself. I can't figure out why, but it can't be as important as your art. Maybe you're not a true artist. Maybe you're just another sad girl thinking she's something she's not."

His words had hit home, echoed in my ears then and now, as though my past was standing next to me. As if I'd been transported back to a place I'd never wanted to be.

At that moment, Meghan came into the quiet room and put her arm through Jared's purposely. Possessively, even, as she smiled at my discomfort, but it quickly dropped from her face when she looked me up and down and noticed my hands fisted at my sides.

"This is Meghan," Jared said, oblivious to our tension—or pretending to be.

"This was a private conversation," I pointed out.

"He tells me everything," Meghan informed me smugly.

That wasn't true—I saw the denial in Jared's eyes that she was refusing to see. But that didn't mean she wasn't smart enough to put two and two together, if not tonight, then soon.

She smirked, as though reading my mind.

How long had she been hanging out by the door, listening to our conversation? Long enough, I felt, to have way too much of my private information. "We're done here," I announced to him. I took a step toward her and she moved back behind Jared, which had me smirking this time.

Sometimes, violence was the answer—the only answer.

To an outsider, we could be talking about anything, I supposed. I kept my voice level, my expression neutral so as not to give anything away in front of the crowd mere feet away. Whether or not this would fool Ann Maslow, who I noticed watching us through the doorway, was anyone's

SHELTER ME

guess, but she wasn't stupid. This was how gossip started, and whether or not the gossip put me at the center of Jared's book or in his bed, it didn't really matter. I was standing between Jared and Meghan, and I was obviously angry.

Jared followed my gaze to Ann and he immediately put on his publicity face. Meghan locked her fingers around his biceps and smiled too as he said, "Ann, are you enjoying the party?"

"Very much. I didn't mean to interrupt—"

"Bullshit," I muttered into my drink, and I'm sure she heard. Meghan glared at me for not playing along but, as everyone knew, I wasn't good at that.

"But I knew I'd have to corner you to get any kind of exclusive quote," Ann finished with a glance in my direction. "I didn't know you and Ryn Taylor knew one another."

I glanced at Jared. We hadn't come up with any kind of cover story. I knew the truth was always better, but in this case, the truth was way too damaging. "We just met tonight. Brayden thought I'd enjoy this party," I said brightly, then raised my drink in a toast-like fashion to Jared. And then I downed it and walked away.

I had bigger things to be scared of than Ann Maslow. So did she—she just didn't know it.

I walked away from the three of them—they deserved each other—and I immediately ran into Lucas. He'd been waiting just outside the room holding a plate of food, and I wondered if he could sense the tension.

If the look on his face was any indication, the answer was yes. But all I could do was lean on him and say, "This has been such a shitty day." But then I looked up into his dark blue eyes and added, "Except for the shower."

"Let's get out of here and take another one, then," Lucas said, and began to steer me out of the apartment.

"Hey, wait up, Ryn."

Lucas and I both turned at the sound of Jared's voice and then Jared was handing me a copy of his book. "I'm so glad you came. I think you'll enjoy it. Really."

He walked away before I could say anything. I wanted to drop the book on the floor but I needed to read it, had to know what I was up against, so I clutched my new, made-up past against my chest and let Lucas take me home.

11

MY HEAD WAS SPINNING. I could barely breathe, but I forced myself to put one foot in front of the other and let Lucas guide me out of Jared's building and into his car. I was still clutching Jared's book to my chest, hating to touch it but unable to let it go.

"What the hell's going on with you, Ryn?" Lucas was asking. When I looked at him, he'd reached over me and pulled the seatbelt over my arms, and the book, since I hadn't been responding.

Maybe I was in shock. I nodded, or at least I think I did. Lucas stared at me for another long moment and then he took off. I didn't bother to ask him to take me to my apartment. He wouldn't—not with the state I was in, and it didn't matter, really. As long as I had the book, which I had to read immediately. I needed to know what I was up against.

I closed my eyes and conjured up the vision of Meghan threading her arm through Jared's. What if Jared told Meghan about my past? And even if he hadn't, it wasn't that much of a leap for her to put two and two together, not after she'd seen my interaction with Jared.

"What's got you all fucked up?" Lucas asked finally, once he'd settled me inside his apartment. I barely remembered him leading me inside or sitting me down at the table, but here I was, still clutching the damned book.

I swallowed hard and put it down on the table between us. Lucas frowned and stared at it and I knew I'd have to spell it out, at least a little bit. "The premise…the seventeen-year-old girl with amnesia. He said it wasn't based on anyone he knew, but he's lying."

Lucas's expression hardened. "Jesus Christ. That fucking bastard. This book…this is about you?"

"I don't know how much. Jared said he made up a past for me, so not entirely," I managed. But I couldn't deny that the story was based on the past—or the lack of—I'd told him about, however loosely. He'd taken liberties, but it wouldn't take much to connect us…and anyone who did some digging would discover my life seemed to begin at age seventeen. Yes, Susan and Arnold did their best to fashion a past—I was adopted post-Katrina after being orphaned, and my records were destroyed in the hurricane. I became a fault of the system, a child who fell through the cracks, thankfully into a wonderful situation.

And suddenly, I wanted to tell Lucas Caine everything, and more than I'd ever wanted to tell Jared. Back then, I'd been stupid, thought we'd gotten close because were both artists. Because we'd had great sex.

"I trusted Jared. I was young. Stupid. In love."

He pressed his mouth into a firm line. "He's an asshole."

"Yes. And I expected too much from him. It's my fault too."

"Tell me what I need to know to keep you safe."

"What makes you think my past is something I need to be kept safe from?"

"Why else would you be so torn up over Jared's book?" He stared at me. "Do you not remember anything about your past?"

My mouth went dry, my throat tightening painfully even as I managed, "Not even my name."

He frowned. "When do your memories start?"

"How much time do you have?"

"For you, Ryn? The rest of my goddamned life."

Fortified with a full bottle of whiskey, water and an ice bucket, Lucas sat with me in his big bed, with the lights low enough so I could talk without seeing every change of expression on his face. I knew he wouldn't pity me, but just in case…

"Brayden knows about this. And Susan and Arnold, they took me in, after…" I trailed off, realizing the only place to start was at the beginning. Lucas remained patiently waiting, watching me. "My first memory is waking up in the hospital. I didn't know who I was. I didn't know why I was there. I didn't know anything. I should've been terrified. Maybe the pain meds took the edge off." The whole experience of those first weeks was hazy. "I remember feeling like wherever I was, I was much safer than where I'd been." And there had been comfort in knowing I could trust my gut, even in those very early stages of 'Who the fuck am I?'

After a while, that question became less important than the fact that whoever I was might be what was holding me back from living the way I needed to. It ultimately forced my hand.

"At first, the doctors thought I was taking too much pain medication and that was messing with my memories. They knew I'd suffered a trauma—a brain injury—but from what they told me, it shouldn't have affected my memory."

"But obviously, something did," Lucas said quietly.

I nodded. "After about a week, the doctors consulted a shrink, and they began sharing with me how bad my condition was when I was first brought in. What had happened to me." I took a shaky breath and told Lucas about the surgeries that had been performed on me. "They placed my age at seventeen. They were corrective surgeries to my face. Plastic surgeries. To this day, I'm not sure if I was beaten so I could have reconstructive surgery on purpose or..." I shrugged.

I didn't know what to think, and I never delved too deeply on this part. It was too disturbing to know that the person looking back at me in the mirror wasn't someone I could ever hope to recognize.

And that maybe that was the point. "I have scars," I managed.

He swallowed hard, reached out his hands as if to feel for them without realizing he was doing so. When he did realize it, he pulled back, but I caught his wrists and tugged his hands forward... brought his fingertips up to stroke the thin, well-healed scars behind my ears.

"How…" He cleared his throat. "How different did you look?"

"The doctors aren't sure if I had a full reconstruction or not." I just shrugged. "It's not like I remember." He was still gently stroking the sides of my face behind my ears and all I could do was continue. "I was still healing, but since I was young…well, they didn't know how long I'd been healing for, you know? I was out, but they didn't know if I'd been kept drugged to stay out or if I'd been in a coma and the drugs were on board for other, life-saving purposes, or if the drugs and the surgery caused the memory loss. Hell, they can't even tell me if I painted before the memory loss— they think my talent might've been brought on by a traumatic brain injury. I had a ton of rehab in the hospital, with physical, occupational and speech therapy, but because of where the injury was, and my age, I made rapid progress. The weird part was coming back to society and knowing general things—like knowing about the television and how to drive a car—but not knowing about my own life. The doctors weren't sure if my memory loss was because of the TBI or if it was a kind of hysterical amnesia, but they kept telling me that if they had to guess, it was always the latter. They surmised that whatever happened to earn me the TBI was so horrible that my own brain wanted to protect me from it." I stopped my sudden tirade and drew in a deep breath.

He leaned his forehead in to touch mine. "Trouble, Ryn. So much fucking trouble."

"I know. I'm sorry."

He assured me, "I'm not."

I managed a small smile before continuing. "I was in the hospital for a while. A month, I think. No one was sure what to do with me. Missing Persons had no records of me, and I got the feeling that the police were wary of digging too deeply. And the US Marshals got involved."

He looked at me sharply. "Are you in witness protection?"

"No. I mean, not really. I was given a past, but there wasn't any reason for them to take me on. And I was already aged out of foster care, technically, but one of the marshals knew this woman who helped with cases of women who needed help. I was a lot different than the women she usually took in, but Susan didn't care."

I told Lucas about Susan and Arnold. Working at the café. The urge to paint that was immediate, even in the earliest stages of healing.

"I was drawing on everything. Napkins."

"I can see that."

I told him about my apartment in the Catskills. About meeting Brayden years later through Susan.

And then I told him about Jared.

At seventeen, I was healed and alive with my art, a wild girl, barely restrained by circumstance. Susan and Arnold knew their hold on me was tenuous and they balanced it well. I'm sure I kept them up nights. I took chances—I was part hermit, part party girl when my art released me for those brief periods of time.

But Jared...he'd come into my life during a period of uncertainty, when Brayden was beginning to sell my paintings for some good money. For a twenty-one year old who'd never had anything like it, the entire experience was odd. I was a paid artist. A recognized one.

I hadn't expected Jared to be jealous, but honestly, he had been. I'd expected too much from him—his first deal had been good but mine had far exceeded his, and after I'd spilled my guts about my past, he was gone.

I'd never expected to have to stand across from him, his book—my life—in his hands. And look what he'd done with it—exposed it to the world. The old feelings rushed back—they were all about how bad he used to make me feel. How inadequate. How had I ever thought I'd been in love with him? Or worse yet, that he loved me? He loved to put me down and for the months we'd dated, that's all he'd done.

I'd blamed the artistic temperament. The book he was writing was taking everything from him. It had always been all about him and nothing that he'd done for me.

The differences between him and Lucas were in such stark contrast that I was sick to my stomach just thinking about it…and when I thought about how badly I'd treated Lucas for a while there. Lucas not only seemed to understand the artistic temperament, but he accepted it.

"I'm a big boy, Ryn," he told me after I'd apologized again. "You don't have to apologize for doing what you love. That's what keeps you happy. I want you happy."

I want you happy.

Jared only seemed happy when I was crying or yelling. He'd fed off it like an emotional vampire, letting it fuel him—when he'd upset me enough so I couldn't paint, he could write. It was all so obvious now, but back then, I was so desperate to make him happy. He was my amazing, tortured artist. My soul mate.

Even though I knew he wasn't the man from my pictures…

Lucas interjected. "I'll make sure Jared keeps his mouth shut."

"How?"

"Let me worry about that. Let me worry about

everything," he told me and as much as I wanted that, I couldn't let it happen.

"You don't understand."

"He wrote about personal things from your relationship," he stated.

I hadn't even thought about that. "Well, maybe." Probably. *Asshole scumbag.* "But it's not that simple."

"He wrote about you. How many more confidences could he break?"

I sighed. "I'm more worried about Meghan. If she and Jared are dating...well, she might've overheard me talking with Jared."

"I'll make sure she doesn't pull any shit," Lucas assured me.

I didn't want to know how he'd do any of what he was promising. Or how, since by tomorrow night, the book and movie news would be everywhere, plus the books would be in people's hands. Jared was a minor celeb of the moment and there would be questions, people digging through his past... finding our connection.

My life would never be the same. I'd known that, but I'd never expected this, my secret exposed by someone I'd been so intimate with.

It was horrifying, soul destroying and trust destroying.

At the time, I'd thought I could trust Jared with

anything. My instincts I prided myself on had served me so wrong, betrayed me, failed me so badly, how could I ever think about believing my gut ever again?

And yet, the man who sat next to me…I'd put so much faith into him so quickly. "I'm sorry to bring you this kind of trouble."

Lucas ran the back of his knuckles over my cheek. "I'm sorry to bring up the danger aspects. To sound angry about them. I get that you can't live in a bubble. But you're not well protected."

"Not really, no. But living with a security team wouldn't be living, Lucas."

"I'm sure you've tried different ways to recall your past?"

"Beyond just giving it time? Not really. I tried hypnosis once and it failed." And I wasn't sure if I was grateful or disappointed by that.

He sighed. "Do you think that Susan and Arnold know more than they're telling you?"

"Sometimes. But…"

"Maybe they're protecting you. And themselves."

"Yes," I agreed. And I was equally—and fiercely—protective of both as well. I'd sacrifice my memories for their safety, since Susan especially put my life before hers for so many years. She never came out and told me that, but I knew in my heart it was the truth.

"So you know, in your gut, that there's some reason you need to be protected?" he asked slowly.

"Yes," I whispered. "I've always known that."

"So you've knowingly put yourself in danger by coming to New York and showing your paintings," Lucas said angrily, making me blink myself back to the reality of the future.

"Yes."

"Tell me Brayden's not aware of this." When my only answer to his question was a wince, he muttered, "Jesus Christ, Ryn."

"Brayden's been protecting me for years. He's still protecting me. We figured that if I became well known, it would either bring my past forward or drive it far back into the shadows."

"That's a really big risk."

"I don't look the same."

"How do you know how different you really look?" he demanded, and that stopped me in my tracks.

I'd always assumed my facial reconstruction had been done to hide what I'd once looked like. Had I miscalculated…had the surgery actually been to reconstruct? "I don't want to think about this right now."

"Tough shit. You're in danger. So's Brayden." His eyes blazed fire.

"Probably anyone who spends time with me is in the line of fire," I shot back. "That's what you're really worried about, right?"

He sat back and stared at me. "You think I'm worried about me?" He gave a short, mirthless laugh. "Honey, you have no idea how your past doesn't scare me."

"Then what does?" I asked, because I needed to know. I wasn't sure why I needed to know so badly, but I did.

For a long moment, I wasn't sure he'd answer. When he finally did say, "The way I fell for you," I stood and moved into his lap. He gathered me into his arms and held me there against him, and for the first time in a very long time, I felt completely, utterly safe.

I slept for a little while, all the emotion of the evening taking over better than any sleeping pill. But all that emotion needed more of an outlet than I'd given it, and I found myself standing on the beach in the dark. I heard the violence of the waves, the crack of thunder that broke above my head right after the flash of lightning illuminated the house I faced.

The house I'd been painting. I walked closer to

it in the dark. When the sky lit up again, I saw the blood smeared on the siding, the porch.

I screamed. And I didn't stop.

"Ryn, come on—wake up. You're safe. Come on, sweetheart…you're safe."

Lucas's deep voice crooned to me through the storm and finally—*finally*—I was able to surface. I croaked, "I'm okay." *So far from it.*

"You are," he reiterated.

I sat up, the sheet wrapped loosely around me. "Sorry—"

"Don't be. You've been through hell and back." He rubbed my shoulders, handed me water.

I took several deep breaths and stared out the window into the night. I didn't want to talk about the dreams, the nightmares. Not tonight. But one thing I didn't doubt was that I needed protection.

From who, though?

Maybe from myself. "I need to tell you something else. Something more immediate. I've been getting flowers."

His eyes narrowed. "From Jared?"

"What? No." But I'd never actually considered that. Jared knew my sparse memories, so would he be trying to freak me out to coincide with his book-to-movie adaptation?

"Then who?" Lucas prompted.

"I don't know."

"Ryn…"

I took a deep breath and started at the beginning. "At first, I assumed they were from Bray. I wanted them to be from him."

"How do you know they're not?"

"Because he brought me other flowers." When Lucas looked confused, I clarified. "Someone's bringing in daffodils…and then taking them away."

Instead of scoffing in disbelief, Lucas's expression hardened. To my ultimate relief, he not only believed me, but was angry on my behalf, telling me, "You're not going back to your apartment."

"Lucas, I need to know who's doing this." I heard the danger bells ringing as I pulled back just short of blurting out the whole truth.

"You want to come face to face with whoever's breaking into your place?"

"Yes. Because they're connected to my past. At least, they might be."

He glossed over that for a second. "Or maybe it's a stalker who likes pretty artists." That was something I hadn't considered. "Now tell me what Turner has to do with this?"

"At first, he said he was investigating my stolen painting for insurance purposes," I explained. "But then he seemed more interested in you.

Specifically, warning me away from you."

His expression didn't change this time, but I swear, his eyes darkened. "You let Brayden deal with him. He calls, you don't answer."

"That's what Brayden told me to do."

"Well look at that—Brayden and I agree on something." He paused. "Can you sleep?"

I shook my head. Sleep was the last thing my body asked for now with such close proximity to his. The ache between my legs intensified.

My nipples tightened against the soft cotton of my tee. He circled one with his thumb before flicking the tip hard enough to send a jolt of pleasure to my sex. I fought—failed—to stifle a moan, arched into him, wanting skin brushing skin.

He tugged my tee off, then slid down my body, painting me with kisses. My body shuddered with an erotic charge

This would be the first time I'd be with Lucas as the girl with no memory.

He slid down my body, pressed his face between my legs and licked my cleft through my underwear. I shivered. I was ready to give myself over to his rough touch. There was no way it wouldn't be good.

He slid my underwear off, his tongue finding an inexorable rhythm. My fingers pressed against his shoulders, running along the ink because I'd memorized it. The tension built in my belly from the friction, my climax a slow, delicious build until I looked down and saw him, watching me.

I shattered.

12

AS THE SUN ROSE, I started to draw on a pad of paper I'd found on Lucas's bedside table. He stirred an hour later and found me scribbling furiously.

"Don't move," I told him and he simply blinked and stayed still, falling back to sleep for a bit until I put the paper down, exhausted.

"Do I get to see it?" he asked.

"I thought you were sleeping."

"Hard to sleep when you're being watched," he pointed out.

"You did a good job of faking it," I said, disgruntled as I showed him the pad. "Sorry, I used all your paper. When I need to draw…"

"It's fine." He flipped through the pages. "You're amazing. You have to know that."

"I know I love to draw. That's all I need," I said

quietly. "Plus, you're a good subject."

"You just like me naked."

"There is that." I stretched and he caught me and pulled me down with him.

"Listen, I can move your painting stuff here if you'd feel better about it."

I studied his face. "I wouldn't mind having some of it here, but I can't move here. I can't just give up all my freedom because of Jared…or whatever else is out there."

He nodded, like he'd expected my answer. "You've met Grant before."

"Yes."

"I'm going to have him come over to wire your apartment."

"It's already alarmed."

"This is different. This would let me or Grant or you and Brayden check on rooms in your place whether you're there or not. It's a different level. I can do the hallway too."

That would help me feel better. It would be like looking over my shoulder without having to actually look over my shoulder.

I knew Lucas and Grant worked security together, but I had my suspicions that it was more than simply installing alarms. Lucas never elaborated on his work or travels. I didn't push, because part of me didn't want to know. He worked at night, fought like a cross between street kid and pro. I'd thought about asking Brayden for more specifics about what Lucas did, but maybe he'd be too honest…or not honest enough.

"And after Grant's done, I think you need to sit down with Brayden and talk to him about all of this."

One glance at my texts told me Brayden had learned the contents of Jared's book, no doubt thanks to Lucas. "You've spoken with Bray?"

"Yes. I told him you were okay. But he wants to hear it from you. And he's concerned as to why I'm having Grant wire your place." Lucas poured me another cup of coffee. "Here's your last bit of procrastination. Then you've got to tell Brayden about the flowers and about being followed, okay? He deserves to know."

I was dreading telling Brayden. I knew he'd feel betrayed that Lucas knew about what was happening with me before he did…and that there was no way he'd like that I revealed everything to Lucas.

Brayden would feel betrayed, but at this point, I doubted he'd be surprised. "Let's go to Brayden's apartment first—I want to talk to him now."

Lucas agreed, but wouldn't let me go alone. So when the three of us—me, Lucas and Grant—ended up outside Brayden's door, Brayden wasn't exactly sunshine-and-roses welcoming.

He also wasn't alone, which, for some reason, seemed to annoy the hell out of Grant. I mean, it wasn't the most comfortable situation to have a strange man coming out of Brayden's bedroom having obviously just showered and dressed, and since Brayden stood in front of us in sweatpants and wet hair, the picture wasn't hard to paint.

Except the guy wasn't Zack. I crossed my arms and Brayden muttered, "Don't start," at me and then, "See you around," to the guy, who said, "Call me," as he slid around us and left.

"Sorry to interrupt," Grant said. "But this is important."

"I don't even fucking *know* you," Brayden shot back as Lucas stayed strangely silent, watching the interaction with interest.

"Bray, this is—"

"Lucas's hired hand," Brayden finished and I swear I heard a growl come from deep and low in Grant's throat, although when I turned, Grant's expression was neutral.

"He's my business partner," Lucas broke in as if to settle the stalemate.

"Didn't realize we were having unscheduled

meet-and-greets," Brayden muttered.

"Please, Bray, let me explain." Something in my tone made Brayden stop his stonewalling.

"You okay?" he asked, his voice low.

"I am. But…" I paused. "I need to tell you something."

"About the book?" Brayden asked.

"No. About the flowers."

"Why don't you let me go downstairs and check out your place while you finish up?" Grant suggested.

"Why don't we all go?" Brayden snapped irritably, grabbing his shirt and shoes and padding toward his door. He held it open and ushered us all out.

It was a quiet, uncomfortable elevator ride even though we were only going down a single floor. Brayden was the one to open my door, shut off the alarm and survey the apartment first. Grant went in next, room to room like he was checking for something…or somebody. That made me nervous as hell, but he came out of my bedroom and said, "All clear. How does everything look, Ryn? Anything out of order?"

"No flowers," I said hesitantly after I scanned the areas I could see. "At least not in here."

Lucas followed me through the rest of the apartment. I was relieved to see everything in place and nary a daffodil in sight.

"There is one thing, though," I said slowly, pointing to a grouping of my newer paintings, which didn't include *Man in Trees*. "These are out of order."

"What do you mean?" Grant asked.

"I put them in a certain order last night and it's different now," I explained.

"Are you absolutely sure? You remember the exact order?" Grant persisted.

"Are you calling her a liar?" Brayden broke in.

"I know it sounds weird, but I definitely remember how I leave my paintings. I do it purposely. There's a method to it." A method to trying to regain my past, I almost said, but I was pretty sure they were all thinking it.

"Is this the first time this happened?" Lucas asked now.

"Yes." I crossed my arms, wanting to study this new order but knowing I wouldn't be able to concentrate with Grant and Lucas here. Instead, I took pictures of the new order and walked away to let Grant figure out the wiring.

"You seem pretty calm for someone who had someone in here touching her art," Lucas said.

"Someone's trying to send me a message. The daffodils were a message too," I said. "Good or bad…I need to know."

Brayden spent the afternoon stomping around my apartment while Grant wired every inch of the place in a completely unobtrusive manner, which I guess was the whole point. He glared at me, Grant and Lucas and I showered to avoid part of that wrath. I heard them all arguing while I was in the shower, but I couldn't make out much over the running water and I didn't bother trying.

I was emotionally exhausted. Lucas was right—it was time to tell Brayden what I'd been hiding, and I knew my best friend would be angry but ultimately forgive me. Telling him would be the easiest part, and that's what worried me most. Because from here, nothing was solved. Nothing was safe.

"I showed Brayden how to use the system," Grant told me. "I can show you too, if you'd rather—"

"I said I can show her," Brayden bit out from behind him and Grant stiffened visibly.

"It's okay," I said with apology in my tone. "Thanks for doing all of this."

"It's no trouble," Grant said.

Lucas gave me a smile, and a kiss that promised he'd see me later. They left, and Brayden locked the door behind them and immediately used the code on the alarm pad.

"It's the same code," he explained. "The only difference is that you can use different numbers to let Grant and Lucas know if you're okay or if you think someone's following you."

Brayden took the time to explain the system to me first, putting my safety ahead of everything. Then he looked at me and said, "They want to wire my apartment too. I'm letting them do it now."

"Good." Relief coursed through my body. "I'm so sorry, Bray. I didn't think about how my past could affect you too. And then I wasn't sure if I was imagining things, especially after the first flowers disappeared. I felt like I was going crazy. It was right before the show. I called Dr. B and he said it could've been a stress fugue state, like what happens when I paint…" I trailed off. "I was going to tell you about being followed, but it happened right before the party and then…"

"And then," Brayden echoed. "You shouldn't have to explain to me. I'm not one to lecture. Hell, I'm no one's idea of a role model."

"You're mine."

He side-eyed me. "Shade, Ryn?"

"Not at all," I took his hand in mine. "You're a successful business owner. I can't believe how much you accomplished from sheer will. When you explained it to me, without me asking and after I'd shared my past...you didn't have to. You trusted me as much as I trusted you. I knew then you'd be a friend for life."

"Ride or die, babe." Brayden squeezed my hand. "I can spot the broken ones. I can't always fix them though."

"That's not your job."

"It's not?"

I smiled, because I knew, underneath the joke, he was more than half serious. "You gave me a chance. You let me fix myself. That's the only way this works." I paused. "You've always given me the space to find my own way. I needed that."

He sighed. "I want to protect you from the world. I understand Lucas's need to do so."

I blinked. "You're actually agreeing with Lucas?"

"World must be coming to an end."

"Want to talk about Zack?"

"Not really."

"I thought..."

"It's easy," Brayden broke in, then conceded, "Sometimes. We don't have a commitment. We don't want one."

"I believe you don't want one, not from him but..." I shook my head. "What happened between you and Grant?"

"What? Nothing," he protested.

"Right." I stared at him he threw his hands up in the air.

"He's a good-looking guy."

"Very," I agree.

"You didn't trust me enough," Brayden blurted out, like he'd been trying to hold it inside and couldn't any longer.

He looked so hurt that tears came to my eyes. "I didn't want to worry you."

"Didn't want to worry me?" he echoed, his tone one of complete disbelief. "You're shitting me, right? You think I haven't worried about you every single day since I met you? You think I haven't worried that I've been exposing you to terrible things by asking you to share your art with the world? You don't think I have sleepless nights over this shit, Ryn?"

No, I hadn't realized just how worried Brayden was. It sounded like he might be more so than I was. "I'm sorry. At first, I thought...shit. I thought it was me being stressed. And crazy. And I thought, maybe I was taking pills without realizing it. Maybe I was that crazy artist everyone was writing about."

"If you are, I wouldn't care. You're Ryn. You're my best goddamned friend, okay?" he said roughly. "And we don't keep secrets like this from each other."

"I won't anymore, okay? I promise." I paused. "I know you said you understand Lucas's protectiveness…but you still don't trust him, do you?"

"I don't trust him," he agreed. "But I do trust you."

"Then trust me that I think I can trust him."

Brayden looked skeptical. "I'll try, babe."

"That's all I ask."

After Brayden and I talked, we decided that I should read Jared's book while he ordered dinner. He'd already read most of it and having him here while I speed read through it would help me immensely.

"You're going to be pissed," he warned.

"I'm already pissed," I pointed out, and opened the cover with a sigh.

I practically read through my fingers, not really wanting to see the words on the page and cringing through the parts of my life that he did happen to use—basically, that constituted the entire first half—and then saw what he'd made up for my past.

God, it would be nice if this fairy-tale horror

story was the truth; would be even better if Jared was psychic or a detective…and I had to admit, it'd make a great, sappy movie.

This wasn't my life at all, especially not the neat wrapping. I'm not sure how I knew that, but I did.

Well, at least I could be certain that Jared wasn't a true part of my past. His book and his movie were agitating whoever wanted to make sure I retained my amnesia, but it wasn't the truth.

If I wanted it, I had to make sure I remained a target. I had to make myself vulnerable.

It certainly wouldn't be the first time. I slammed the book shut and looked up at Brayden.

He shook his head. "The book, I mean it's you, but it's not…"

"It's not anything I didn't tell him," I finished and slumped down to the couch in misery.

"Hey, he dazzled you at first." Brayden sat next to me. "No one's going to know it's you."

"At least he's changed artist to writer. Because he's an egomaniac." I sat up. "Oh my God, he turned me into him!"

Brayden laughed.

"It's not funny," I told him before dissolving into hysterical laughter, the kind that you had to do or else you'd cry instead. We rolled around on the couch until our sides hurt while we absorbed the truth.

"You could pretend you think this version's the truth," Brayden said finally. "Come out publicly. Say you're grateful. Pretend to be with him."

I thought about that. It might make whoever was coming for me back off but… "Then I'll never know the truth."

"Sometimes the truth isn't worth knowing."

IN THE DAYS FOLLOWING the party, the papers were all about Jared and his book, the subsequent movie and its casting. Gabrielle Weston, the actress I'd met at Jared's book party, had gotten the part of…me. That was almost a relief, in a weird sort of way. The guy Jared picked to play himself was a handsome star who appeared like he could be as big of a jerk as Jared himself. Thankfully my name hadn't been mentioned, but I was still suspicious of Ann Maslow and assumed she was digging into any connection she could find.

If she went upstate to the Catskills, Susan and Arnold would get wind of it immediately, and our small town would effectively cut the investigation off. That was the benefit of living in a place where everyone knew you.

They knew me, but they didn't know my background. Even so, I was one of their own, and any stirring up trouble would be met with the cold shoulder.

Jared was the one who couldn't be trusted. I was still most worried about him, and about Lucas attempting to shut him down, but I threw myself into work so I didn't obsess about it. I knew Lucas read the book as well, and although he must've had questions, he was good about not asking them. He attempted to keep my mind free of anything but art and him, and for the moment, I was okay with that.

But two weeks later, after most of the news of the movie was dying down (and would gear up again once production began, I realized), Brayden called me from the gallery.

"Gabrielle came in looking for you," he told me.

"She did?" I still had her card, of course, but assumed that her urging me to call had been nothing but polite party chatter.

"She didn't have your number and you hadn't called her. Anyway, I took her number again and told her you'd call. She seemed really nice."

"She bought more art, didn't she?" I asked cynically.

"Yes, but that's not why I think she's nice,"

Brayden countered. "She seemed like she needed a friend."

"You don't think it's dangerous to talk to her?"

"I've considered that. It might be, but it's also a way to keep up on what's happening without having to approach Jared."

"I don't want to use her, Bray," I protested.

"Well, you should be able to figure out fast enough if she's using you. If she's not…well, Ryn, you deserve to have friends, right?"

"I have you."

"Always, babe. But this is your time to shine. Gabrielle loves your art. She'd be a good supporter."

"And I like her," I said softly. "Okay, I'll call her."

"Good. Let me know what happens."

I wasn't sure Lucas would be as enthusiastic as Brayden was, but I also knew he'd never stop me from making this call. I dialed the number nervously. I didn't know how to make friends. Brayden came to me, as did Lucas. But I wasn't good with women, as evidenced by Meghan.

"She's not Meghan," I told myself firmly, right before Gabrielle answered. "Hey, I heard you were looking for me."

"I'm so glad you called. Listen, can you meet me for lunch?" she asked. "I'm close to the gallery—I saw some of your new pieces."

"Cool. And sure, okay." I wrote down the

address and met her at the restaurant about twenty minutes later. It was well past lunchtime and she was seated all the way in the back.

She jumped up when she saw me. "Hey you," she said, then leaned in to give me a hug. "Oh, sorry—maybe you're not a hugger."

"It's okay. It's good to see you again."

"You too. I don't know…there was just something about you that I felt really comfortable with. I hope it's okay that I asked for you to get in touch," she said, motioning for me to sit.

"No, it's cool. I wouldn't have bothered you otherwise."

"Trust me, I don't give my number out to many people. Or any people," she confessed.

"Me neither." We smiled at each other across the table and I immediately knew she wasn't going to be pumping me for information—at least not at Jared's behest.

Just then, the waitress came by with a tray, laden with food. "Can I get you something to drink?" she asked as she put down plates of food.

"I ordered some appetizers and stuff. We're in between lunch and dinner, but I know the owners," Gabrielle explained.

"Sounds good." I ordered a Diet Coke and realized I was starving. "I haven't congratulated you yet about getting the part," I told her, in between bites of fried food she confessed she shouldn't be eating.

She smiled, but it didn't quite reach her eyes. "I knew I was right for it. I hope that doesn't sound conceited, but sometimes, you just know." It was then I noticed that she looked tired. She was beautiful—naturally so, and she could get away with lack of sleep and makeup, but this was more than that. And I wasn't going to question her about it, because this was our first lunch, but after a brief moment's hesitation, she asked, "There weren't any paparazzi outside, right?"

"None that I saw."

"Good." She took a sip of water. "Lately, they've been following me with a vengeance. The price of fame, I realize. I know you've dealt with them recently too."

I rolled my eyes in commiseration. "Not fun."

"Not at all," she said softly, and her entire countenance changed, as if she dropped the 'it's all good' act entirely.

I leaned forward on my elbows, concerned. "What's wrong?"

She sighed. "God, I'm the worst new friend ever, right? New friends are supposed to talk about happy stuff."

"So pretend we're not new friends."

"It feels like we're not, right?" she asked and I

nodded. "It's just that, I feel like I can talk to you. Which is weird because I never feel like that, even about people I've known forever."

"I'm a good secret-keeper," I told her and hi, understatement of the year.

She lowered her voice purposefully, like it was a new habit she was cultivating. "I'm thinking of giving up the part."

I couldn't hide my surprise. "What? Why?"

She spread her fingers helplessly, palms up toward the sky. "I have a past."

The weight of her statement settled over me, hot and heavy. "We all do."

She shook her head hard. "Not like mine. I know it's hard to understand, but trust me…"

All this time I'd been so worried about my own past, about Gabrielle seeing right through me, that I'd been blind to the fact that everyone had their own shit. Everyone had something to hide. Just because I was caught up in my own drama didn't mean that everyone else was.

I needed to get my head out of my ass. I leaned forward and took Gabrielle's hands in mine. "Tell me what I can do to help. Because there's no way you can give up this opportunity. I don't know you well, but I've got to bet you've worked toward this kind of success for years. You've sacrificed and struggled. Part of this is fear of exposure, yes, but part is also pure and simple fear."

She stared at me and finally the hint of a smile ghosted along her lips. "I guess you'd know, right? Based on your first show and all."

"And that turned out…great." I managed to balance the last word with enough brightness and sarcasm to make her burst out laughing.

And then I joined her.

"Ah, I needed that," she said, wiping her eyes carefully with the pads of her fingers. "I've been too much inside my own head today."

"Yeah, I know what that's like." I gave her a sympathetic frown. "Want a drink?"

"Desperately."

Two shots of tequila later, we turned to sipping the amber liquid on the rocks and she was confessing that reporters had been threatening to look into her past if she didn't grant them exclusive, behind the scenes interviews on Jared's movie.

"Are there people in your past who will talk?" I asked carefully.

"Aren't there always?" She took a sip of her drink and winced. "I'm too much of a lightweight for this." She paused. "Is that why you didn't say much in your interviews?"

"Yes," I said honestly.

"You know they won't ever give up."

"I know that too." I wanted that, but it wasn't the time to share it. Yet.

"I think that's why I was drawn to you. Because I feel like you understand secrets, and you do it well. I need to learn that." She sighed. "You'd think I'd have come to terms with this a while ago."

"You were being superstitious. Not counting your chickens."

"I guess." She slid her drink away. "I guess I'll just have to deal with it when it comes out."

"Won't your manager handle it?"

"If I chose to tell him." Her mouth curved in a wry smile. "In this business, it's hard to trust."

"I get that. What about Jared?" I asked carefully.

"What about him?"

"Maybe…he could write your memoirs?"

She laughed a little. "I barely have a career."

"It could be an article," I pointed out. "Who better to talk about this with than the man who's going to put you on the map?" God, I couldn't believe how crazy this was, but Jared definitely had experience in spinning things. "You could make sure you have control over the article too. Come up with the way you want to come across. Surely, Jared would understand."

She nibbled her bottom lip for a second. "It's not a bad idea…but Jared? He's very…"

"Self-absorbed? Out for himself?" I said

and she nodded. "Draw up paperwork. Or find someone else. There's got to be someone for hire for this kind of thing."

"You're right, Ryn. I've got to take control of it myself."

I wondered if maybe I should be taking my own advice. I clinked my glass to the one she'd set down and finished my drink, for both our sakes.

Lucas and I ended up in bed almost immediately after he came by, sometime after two in the morning. I was covered in paint and he ended up the same. We showered off sometime before sunrise and had coffee before we'd even slept.

I loved this upside-down life of mine. Loved that I had someone to share it with. Lucas seemed to thrive in this mixed-up world of nights and days the same way I did.

"Are you done working?" he asked.

"I think so." But in reality, I never knew. If the urge hit, I'd leave the bed and start drawing or painting. "I met with Gabrielle today. She came by the gallery and wanted me to have lunch with her."

"You knew she got the part," Lucas said, letting

me know that he'd been following the gossip closely, and certainly not for his love of movies or tabloids.

"I knew. She's freaked out."

"Why?"

"The fame. The fact that people will dig into her past."

"And she's got one?"

"Enough of one that she was thinking of giving up the part. I told her to find a way around it, told her to figure out a way to tell her own story before anyone else did," I said.

"You're a good friend, Ryn." He paused. "Sounds like you've got a lot in common."

"I'm being careful. And no, I don't think she's working for Jared—not like that," I told him. "She seemed really scared."

"She's an actress," he pointed out.

"And I've got a gut intuition that I follow," I shot back.

"I'm not trying to make you feel bad or doubt yourself, Ryn. I'm trying to protect you. Let me."

"How?"

"Let me find out about Gabrielle's past. Then I'll know if she's being truthful."

I thought about it for a minute. "Fine. But don't tell me about it, okay?"

"Deal."

I knew Lucas wouldn't share it with the world, but this way, he'd see that Gabrielle was telling the truth and then I could be comfortable in our growing friendship. I might not need a huge group of friends, but having another female in the mix was nice.

"What's really bugging you?"

I shrugged, like it wasn't a big deal, but he knew better. "I just really feel for her."

"Why?"

I bit the words out before they clogged my throat. "I can feel her fear. She's worried she's going to lose something she's worked so hard for." I paused. "I'm sure you can guess my biggest fear."

He sat back. "You're worried that if you get your memories back, you'll lose your art."

Hearing him say it—hearing someone else say it out loud besides me—made the fear both bigger and yet somehow more manageable. Maybe because it was somehow now shared. "Suppose I lose it? Suppose getting my memories means losing whatever creates that art? You said it yourself when you met me." *Protect whatever the hell makes those.*

"I guess it's something you'll have to decide if it's worth chancing…what you want badly enough."

"I don't know what I want that badly," I

confessed. When he raised his brows, I added quickly, "Besides you."

"Better. And don't forget, Ryn, that you're already here, out in the open. I think you've already made your decisions. You're just trying to be at peace with them. For tonight, at least, let's just be." He tugged me down on top of him and we lay on my bed, in the middle of the night, in the rain. And it was perfect, this just being.

How long could things remain perfect? In my estimation, maybe another ten minutes.

14

BRAYDEN AND I WENT out to dinner the following evening, for some bonding time. We also took in a gallery show for another up-and-coming artist, and thankfully there wasn't much press there. I felt bad for the artist, but happy for me, since the last thing I wanted was to be in the paper at the same time as Jared was.

Ann Maslow had been quiet. I wasn't ashamed to say I'd been googling her name in order to keep up on her most recent articles, and there was nothing about me in any of them.

Still, I wouldn't let my guard down. She was too smart to not trust her obvious suspicions, and I had no doubt she was digging for information.

When I got back to my apartment, Brayden came in and made us coffee. When I began to wander over to my canvases, I heard him tell me goodbye and him turning on my alarm for me before he left to go upstairs.

Several hours later, covered in paint and emotionally exhausted, I stood back and surveyed my newest work against the backdrop of some of the older ones I'd taken to studying, particularly some of the *Man in Trees* portraits that I kept out, because they made me feel like I was back in the Catskills. That brought a sense of comfort to me the nights when I needed it most.

Tonight, that sense of comfort grew cold when I realized what I was looking at. I'd set out to work on the commissioned piece—and I obviously had. But it took me several moments to figure out what was wrong. It was almost like a sense of being off balance, as if I was seasick, unable to get my sea legs.

It was nothing like what I'd set out to paint. My mind had overridden everything else but what my muse wanted. Sometimes I looked on it as a gift. Tonight, I was just frustrated.

The house I'd painted was barely recognizable— dark, run-down and frightening, like a haunted house, a place to be avoided rather than revered and worth the amount of money I'd been paid to paint it. The outside was an angry slash of blue, a deep indigo combined with a cut of red in the dark sky that looked unnatural and menacing. The beach in front of it held the angry waves of a storm in progress instead of the tranquil blue waters of the day scene. And all of it was shrouded, as if it was trying to hide from everyone...but especially from me.

The storm echoed what I felt inside as I stared hard at my creation. I looked closer at the yellow and red smudges on the sanded beach and then took a step back as if trying to erase what I'd seen.

Daffodils.

Blood.

Fuck.

Immediately, I moved the four other paintings I'd attempted of the commissioned piece. Each of them hinted at the darkness I'd drawn...each of them represented a different season, three of them set during dusk and this one, black of night.

None of them looked like a fair representation of the photo of the house I was supposed to be painting. All of them looked like puzzle pieces that didn't fit together, had no meaning for me beyond the daffodils scattered on the beach.

Daffodils had shown up in my apartment, but no blood. I had zero memory of this house. Nothing about it reminded me of anything. It didn't jolt my senses.

"None of it fits," I muttered, my frustration practically morphing my words into a growl.

What surprised me was how violent I felt, as if I wanted to reach out and destroy all my paintings. Whoever was leading me to discover my past was doing a piss-poor job of it. And I told them so, in case they were listening. "You're not helping me, and I'm tired of being scared. Asshole."

No one answered, but I felt better, at least. Slightly more in control.

When the phone rang a few seconds later, I picked up Brayden's call.

"I can't sleep—are you working?"

"I'm yelling at the paintings."

"New technique?"

"Something like that." It was only then I realized that something else was wrong, because the *Man in Trees* paintings weren't in the order I'd left them in. I closed my eyes and realized that the three commissioned paintings hadn't been either, but I'd been in too much of a hurry to notice. Now, I moved to put them back where they'd been as I told Brayden, "Someone's been in here."

"Shit." I could hear him leaving his apartment and coming to me. "You're way too laid back about this."

I heard him using the key, walking in until he was staring at my newest painting, which was still front and center, the phone still at his ear. "Fuck me."

"You're not my type," I told him.

He hung up and moved closer. "Who are you and what have you done with Ryn? And what the fuck is this?"

"New painting. I'll show you it with the others in a second. But first, check all of those—there's a new order here. Whoever's breaking in is trying to tell me something."

Together, Brayden and I stared at the paintings. After many long minutes of silence, he said, "Basically, he's saying that your memories are out of order."

"I guess even my dreams are faulty." I pointed to the floor. "They left my *Man in Trees* pieces alone again."

Brayden gave them a hard stare and muttered something about how even psychos had taste.

"I know you don't like them, but they are my best sellers."

"Pretty equal now with the landscapes." He glanced at me. "I couldn't sleep because I got a call from Jared."

"Trying to turn him?" Brayden just stared at me. "Fine. What for?"

Brayden sighed. "He wants to use some of your paintings in the movie." I stared at him, open-mouthed. "Now you understand why I can't sleep. I'm thinking he doesn't know what I know, about anything. But he knows you'll get this message."

Finally, I managed, "What's he trying to do? To see if anyone notices them and makes a connection?" *Anyone* being Ann Maslow.

"He claims he's trying to help your profile."

"Or put me in more danger." I hugged my arms around myself and stared at the dark beach painting. "Do you think this will bring out my past?"

"It might. He might." Brayden shrugged. "But the more people who know…the more protected you are. And speaking of protected, your boyfriend and his minion are supposed to be the best at protection."

"I can call Lucas."

"I'm calling Grant. He gave me his number."

"He didn't give it to you so you could call and yell at him."

"Too fucking bad," Brayden told me, phone to his ear. Grant must've picked up right away because Brayden continued with, "Yeah, your alarms suck because someone broke into Ryn's. What? No, I'm not drunk. Asshole." He hung up. "Grant's on his way. So is Lucas. And Lucas is pissed you didn't call him."

"I was going to, until you had your hissy fit."

Brayden pointed at me. "Don't even."

Lucas looked fierce as he stalked around my apartment, but only after hugging me and making sure I was okay.

I was angry, but I was okay. And very glad he was there.

"Let me take you to my place," he said.

"No—I won't be pushed out. Besides, someone wants me to learn something. So I'm trying to learn."

"No one's learning shit tonight. Not with me here."

That was probably true. Things like this didn't happen when Lucas was here. There were no random flowers appearing or paintings changing order.

Behind me, I heard Brayden and Grant arguing in low voices. Grant told me that no one had broken in but Brayden immediately insisted that Grant's alarm installation was faulty. That wasn't sitting right with Lucas, but Grant was really and truly pissed.

We left Brayden and Grant to sort things out. I'd taken enough pictures of the paintings so I could study the order, but in reality, I knew staring at them wasn't going to help me. Wouldn't it have already?

It was close to four in the morning by the time we got to Lucas's. He'd stopped to pick up food from the diner around the corner, and we both ate our breakfasts in relative silence. I still couldn't bring myself to stop thinking about the commissioned painting.

"Does Brayden know who commissioned the pieces?" Lucas asked after he studied the photos I'd brought along.

"He said it's anonymous. He's got a P.O. Box to send the paintings to and the down payment was cash."

He was on his phone, talking to Grant. "Ask Brayden to give you the P.O. Box for the commissioned painting and run it." He listened for a second and said, "Let me know."

Then he held up the house pictures. "I can scan these and do an image search."

"Okay."

"But maybe you're not ready for that."

He'd read my hesitation too easily. "I want to know, Lucas, but…"

"You want to do it through your own memories," he finished.

"Yes."

He nodded. "I get that. But what if we get a town…or an owner? Just because you have a name, that's not taking away from your possible memories. Maybe that'll trigger it."

"Can I think about it?"

"Yes." He finished his coffee. "You could return the money and say fuck it to the painting."

I could, yes. "It's not about the money. This is the first real memory trigger for me."

He shook his head. "I don't like the idea of you being manipulated."

"I don't either, but if I don't do this now, I'll always be manipulated." I paused. "Can we watch a movie? I'm not tired, but I need to get my mind off this."

Lucas agreed, and for the next two hours we were on the couch, watching an action movie that was so fast-paced I couldn't tear my eyes off the screen.

When it ended, I went to his kitchen to get more coffee. When I came back, he was still in the same place and I took a second to assess him, as if I was going to draw him.

On second thought, I doubled back, grabbed the pen and paper I'd seen on his kitchen counter and did just that, sketching quickly.

Of course, he knew what I was doing, watched me with the half-amused smirk but staying in position.

On first meeting him, he'd seemed arrogant

—sure of himself to the point of cockiness. He was still arrogant, but dressed in old sweats, with bare feet and a ripped T-shirt, I saw something else…

He was prowly, for lack of a better word. And I told him so.

"Prowly?" He narrowed his eyes. "Is that a compliment?"

"It's like you're stalking. Staking your claim. You do it wherever you go."

"Really?"

"Yes," I informed him. "And you do it here, too, even though it's your place. But you do it in a different way, like you're checking what's yours. Strengthening the perimeters. Putting up walls of defenses."

He smiled a little. "Remember, Ryn, you're already inside. Plank's up. Alligators in the moat."

His feet were up on the coffee table. Masculine, beautiful feet. Elegant and graceful, just like him, but I had zero doubt of his ability to leap and lunge and tear someone's throat out.

Instead of scaring me, it made me hot. "There," I said, more to myself than him. I had my sketch. I could paint from this, and most likely from memory but a reminder never hurt.

Lucas brought me home late the next afternoon. We'd been inside the apartment for ten minutes when the doorman buzzed up that there was a flower delivery for me. My stomach was a bundle of nerves until Lucas opened the door and brought in the Gerbera daises.

Not daffodils. And this bouquet was wrapped from the flower shop down the street, and there was a card.

After Lucas read it though, I began to think that I might rather the daffodils when he growled, "It's from your favorite author."

Dammit. I stared at the flowers and mentally cursed Jared.

"So, what does he want?"

"My paintings," I explained. "He called Brayden last night. He wants to use my paintings for an apartment scene in his movie."

"He wants to use *your* paintings in *his* movie?" I could tell Lucas was tamping down his temper. "You know what this means, right?"

"He's either trying to out me or use the threat to get me to lend my paintings, which would mean I'd be outing myself," I said. "So yes, I'm trying to process what to do, or was, until I realized that someone had broken in."

"You can process. I know exactly what to do

with Jared," he muttered.

"But not tonight." I tugged him to me.

"You think seducing me will stop me from tearing his head off?"

"I'm hoping it will."

He frowned slightly. "I think it might."

He took me in front of the flowers, bent me over the table, spread my sex, holding it open so he could lick and lave my most intimate spots.

I gripped the table as his fingers entered me, along with his tongue.

He was as possessive as I was.

15

LUCAS SEEMED TO BE there to protect me from myself…and the others I didn't yet know about. At first, I'd worried about who was going to protect him from me but now I was more concerned about who would protect me from him.

I actually asked him that. After he bit back laughter, he offered, "I could get you a security team."

"Whatever. You're zero help." Still, between him, Grant and Brayden, I was happier, more balanced and getting more done than I ever had, painting-wise. They must've made a pact to keep as much critical news from me as possible, and although I knew it was out there, being shielded was fine by me.

We made a few appearances, mainly for

charity and typically with Brayden and Grant to throw off any questions. It was like going out with my bodyguards, and if I could ignore the angry electricity bouncing between Grant and Brayden, it would've been perfect. Then again, maybe that made it perfect for them.

Lucas was more of a homebody than I was, thanks to our upside-down life, although there were restaurants we could go to at one in the morning that would give us a private dinner.

Beyond that, it was sex and painting and I kept thinking it would end soon, either by him or me. It was both of our MOs to fuck each other and then fuck each other over and yet we weren't doing that. We were digging each other in deeper. There were times he wouldn't call for a day and I'd find myself calling him, realizing he wanted that. He needed to know I would check on him too.

Like when Brayden and I had found each other, Lucas and I were like another lost boy/girl team. He was my lost boy and somehow, even though I knew he had memories, he was more lost than me.

And a hell of a lot wilder. I told him that too.

"I'm domesticated," he insisted.

"Bullshit. Yes, the lions in the wild seem that way, lying contented in the sun. Until called on to do battle."

"Lionesses are fiercer."

I held up my mug in agreement, then took a sip. "Perfect."

There we were, noon on a Friday. What an odd, beautiful life I had.

"Why's that?"

"I get to sleep in. Drink coffee in sweatpants at noon. Stay up all night and get paid to do something I love."

"Everyone should be so lucky."

"Are you?"

"I do what I like."

"And that's what, exactly?"

He gave me a half grin before drinking half his coffee. "You can ask what you want, Ryn."

"Are you broken, Lucas Caine?"

"Sometimes."

"Me too." I stroked his hair. "Maybe all our pieces can fit together. Maybe we were just missing pieces to our puzzle."

"And you said you weren't romantic," he teased.

"I'm not."

Whatever his job, it allowed him to deal with my upside-down days and nights. We'd both work at night and sleep and fuck and eat during the day…and weeks flew by in that manner, some of the easiest times I'd ever had.

He didn't make me feel like I was missing

anything. He filled up the spaces inside of me, or maybe he filled them in so I didn't think about what was missing from my life. It was a similar feeling to what I had with Brayden. I was satisfyingly complete because Lucas made me feel like I was enough, and not just because he didn't question my past. I was secure. Even if I never remembered anything before the age of seventeen, I'd be all right.

Maybe I'd been waiting my whole life for a love like this, not my past memories. Maybe I'd always been complete and I'd just needed someone to share my life with.

"I'm supposed to see Gabrielle tonight," I told him now. She and I had been keeping in touch by text mainly, because she'd been busy with rehearsals followed closely by filming and such.

Now, Lucas looked grim at the mention. "I looked into what Gabrielle's trying to hide," he said finally.

"And it's not good," I finished.

"Definitely not." He shrugged his jacket off and leaned on my kitchen counter. "She's right to be worried."

"Do I have to worry?"

"I know you don't want me to tell you, but…"

I held a hand up. "Don't."

He stared up at the ceiling like he was looking

for patience. He must've found some because he lowered his gaze back to me and said, "Fine. I'll give her some time to come clean with you. Otherwise…"

I re-raised my hand.

"Next time, we're doing this at my place," Gabrielle promised. "I had to run in through the kitchen. It's getting ridiculous."

Jared's book had continued to place number one on the *New York Times* and *USA Today* bestseller lists weeks after its release and news of that and the impending movie were everywhere. I gave up trying not to see it, because no matter how hard Brayden and Lucas tried, it was impossible. "It's just going to get worse," I told her, realizing I was saying it to both of us. When Gabrielle furrowed her brows a little, I admitted, "Jared called. He wants to use my paintings in one of the movie's scenes."

"That's cool…isn't it?" she asked carefully, because my voice had been flat when I delivered the news.

She knew—about me, about the book being about me. I wasn't sure how, but I needed to tell her more than I'd needed to tell anyone. "Jared's book is about me."

She looked around, but we were in a private room and none of the waiters were in here at the moment. "Ryn, don't ever tell anyone that again. Please."

"You don't seem surprised."

She paused, then reached out to touch my arm. "I'm not."

"Jared told you."

"No. You did, but not with words." She sat back. "The other day, I told you I was worried about my past getting out? It's my past that makes me able to read people well. It's a talent I can't seem to break."

"So you're not psychic, then?"

She gave a wry smile. "I've pretended to be, but no." It was my turn to frown, and finally she managed, "My family…they were—are—grifters."

"Thieves?"

"A different kind of thief. They're not hitting banks, but they're playing people who have cash and jewelry. Or anything. They can manipulate people into doing anything, and I grew up watching it. I was born into it, they used to tell me. And I hated every second of it."

She wiped away the trace of a tear angrily, then took a big sip of her wine.

"Gabrielle, you don't have to—"

"Of course I do. It's been so long since I've met

someone real…someone I've connected with. I'm not letting my past get in the way of that. Like I told you the other day, it's going to come out. But if it did before I told you, then you'd never believe in me."

That was probably true. "I guess we're both good secret-keepers."

That earned me a tentative smile. "Early on, I learned how to read people, how to use their own body language against them. I was more in tune with that than anyone else, and I was drawn to you, and to the way you were holding yourself when Jared began his speech. It made me feel like I wanted to save you from whatever it was, or maybe from yourself." She paused. "I'd rather you tell me than share it with the wrong person. And with my past…well, I can see how you might not believe I've got your best interests at heart but—"

I stopped her, putting a hand on her arm. "But you do."

"Yes." She seemed relieved that I believed her. "I'll quit the movie. Really."

"Oh no—you're not going to use me to get out of this part."

She snorted a laugh. "Sure, make my altruistic act seem selfish."

We stared at each other across the table. Both of our demons would come out during the making of this movie. I was becoming more resolved to it by the second, and I think Gabrielle was too.

"Did Jared say he was planning on keeping your secret?" she asked finally.

"He says he won't reveal me, but his timing, just around the time of my show…"

"He planned it, Ryn. They all do. The whole business is calculating."

"We didn't have a D/s thing either," I said. "That's all his imagination. My past is his imagination too."

"Well, at least he kept that to himself."

"He couldn't not," I muttered.

"What do you mean?"

"He made up everything about my past because I can't remember it."

"But in the book… What a complete control freak. He played God with you and your past." She shook her head, looking angry. "I don't know if I can work for him. I mean, no one's happy about it—Jared's pedigree is definitely the only thing keeping the director from strangling him, and we're all hoping he doesn't sink the movie completely. But especially now, knowing what I know, I'm not sure…"

"I didn't tell you this to ruin your opportunity. You need to take this and run with it. Please."

"And what about you?"

"I'm trying to remember. I think someone's trying to help me."

"Is that a good thing?"

"I don't think so. That's why I wanted to tell you. Lucas will probably kill me, but I won't have you in possible danger without your knowledge."

She looked grim. "God, we're a pair, aren't we?"

"I'm just grateful to have people in my life who finally know all about my past," I admitted. "It's nice not having to hide it anymore. That's why I came to New York in the first place. I knew it might draw all of this out. That's why Jared's book doesn't matter to me. He can't hold over me what I'm ready to reveal."

"Do you think Jared might be in danger too?" she asked.

"I don't know," I said honestly. "I don't really care, either."

She smiled. "I'm going to give an interview about my past. An exclusive. Like you said, my manager thought it could only help me. Plus, I'm from a family of grifters, but I'm not one myself. Not since I was much younger."

"When are you doing the interview?"

"Next week. But it won't air immediately. They'll do lots of teasers for it for the next month as filming progresses. It'll be part of the buzz." She used air quotes around the word buzz and rolled her eyes as she did so. "It's show business." She managed a smile, but there was worry behind her eyes. "My manager said I'm going to blow up."

We both knew her life was going to change one thousand percent, first when it was announced and then when the movie came out—her entire existence would be under a microscope.

"Are you ready for all that?" I asked.

"I'll never be." Gabrielle shrugged. "But I want fame and fortune. In return, to have all the doors open for me or give up everything, my dream. There's middle ground for sure, but I'm too competitive for it." Then she paused, and her tone turned heavy. "If I'm under scrutiny, Ryn, and we're friends…"

"Don't."

"I have to. I'll back away from you. Won't mention you at all. Your secret is safe with me. Maybe it's better if we don't—"

"What? If you let me hide again? First of all, Jared won't. And I don't want to. I wouldn't have come to New York and made a spectacle of myself if I'd wanted to hide."

"You definitely did do that," she said gently. "You're probably the first real person I've met in forever. I'm not just letting that go."

"Me neither," I said honestly.

We sat there tonight, two women whose lives

were just about to change and probably by the time we saw each other again. But for those hours, we were two girls from small towns, enjoying the food and warmth we were showered with. We weren't jaded enough not to enjoy it.

We clinked glasses.

"To being on the verge," she said. "And having someone watching your back so you don't get pushed."

"I'll definitely drink to that."

She glanced to the side. "Your bodyguards are here." I looked up to see Grant and Brayden. I sighed, but she waved them in. "We've got a lot of dessert."

Brayden wasted no time in coming in. Grant rolled his eyes but let himself be coaxed.

I noticed the fresh hickey on Grant's neck. Gabrielle noticed too, and made a 'we so need to discuss this later' face, the same one I made to Brayden.

16

AFTER DINNER, GRANT BROUGHT me back to my apartment as Brayden went to his apartment to grab his things. I knew Lucas and Grant both had to work tonight and they'd obviously talked to Brayden ahead of time about staying with me that evening.

"Are you sure you're all right?" Lucas asked.

"I'm not going to let you miss work to watch me paint," I told him.

"That's not a hardship." He leaned down and kissed me, his tongue stroking the roof of my mouth, taking his time…and it took everything I had not to beg him to stay.

And he knew it, too. "Prowly *and* cocky," I informed him.

"I can't complain about either title," he said as Grant half-dragged him out, muttering something about not being able to fit his ego through the door.

I closed and alarmed the apartment, with Brayden looking over my shoulder, of course. "I've got this."

"Just checking," he said innocently. "Why don't you go do your work?"

"Trying to get rid of me?"

"Never, babe."

In truth, he knew I was itching to paint. I saw him move toward the couch and told him, "Take the bed," but he shook his head, and I realized he wanted to be close to the door. It was, logically, the only way anyone could be entering to move the paintings around, but it seemed like a long shot.

Still, he set up on the couch, the TV on low, and shooed me into my studio.

I went gladly. I had my sketch of Lucas on the couch from last night but I didn't refer to it as I painted on the large canvas. The image of him, protective and prowly, was burned into my brain, down to his feet.

I was smiling as I painted. And when I finally dragged myself to the comfy overstuffed chair in the studio to sketch more, I was exhausted. I fell asleep for maybe twenty minutes. I woke with such a start that I found myself standing straight up like a soldier. I blinked a few times, reached back to steady myself with a hand on the high arm of the chair behind me. It took several minutes for me to realize what I was focusing on—the paintings, of course, but slowly I took them in, left to right. Over and over, I scanned them.

And then I screamed.

Brayden burst inside the room, immediately put his arms around me. I was shaking, but all I had to do was point and he knew.

"Shit." He paled as he stared. "Ryn, I was awake. What the hell?"

"The window," was all I could manage, but he was calling Lucas or Grant or both.

When he hung up, he said, "They said they'll bring the video footage here and we can look at it together."

"I don't know if I want to."

"Then they'll look at it. They don't want to invade your privacy, but checking the footage of your studio is the only way to see who came in," he said quietly.

But when he went to lead me out of the room, I stopped him. "Take pictures of this order. It's different."

He didn't argue, snapped iPhone pictures quickly as I tried to take note of exactly what had changed.

"The *Man In Trees* pictures are involved this time," he said quietly. And they were, spaced in between the commissioned paintings.

I let Brayden lead me out of the studio and into the living room. With a glass of whiskey and a blanket, I curled on the couch with him and waited for Lucas.

Ten minutes later, he and Grant were there. Grant went to talk with Brayden while Lucas came right to me.

"I knew I should've stayed," he told me.

"Brayden was right here, on the couch. He was awake. I was working. Then I fell asleep—not for long and I don't know how it could've happened. He didn't fall asleep. Unless someone came in the window…"

"You know what floor we're on?" Brayden asked from behind us.

Lucas glanced up at him and back at me. "Someone could've worked quietly. If their intent is to freak you out, it worked."

I rubbed my arms. "Definitely."

"The window's wired," Grant said. "No one got into this place without the key and the code."

"Not even you?" Brayden asked.

Grant's eyes narrowed. "Point taken. But we have footage."

"Let's play it," Brayden said.

"Ryn?" Lucas asked.

"I don't want to see it. You guys watch it. Please—I have to know but I don't need to see it."

Lucas nodded. He got up to move near Grant, and Brayden moved to me. "I'll wait with you."

"Thanks, Bray." I grabbed his hand and forced myself not to look over to where the laptop was.

"We can end this once we know," Brayden was saying, but I barely heard it over the noise in my own mind.

And then everything was quiet. Too quiet. I forced myself to look up when Lucas said my name, and he and Grant both looked uneasy.

"What's wrong? Who do you see?" I asked, although my voice sounded far away, even to my own ears.

"We watched it on fast forward so we could look for intruders without invading much of your privacy," Grant told me. "I want to show you what we found."

"Come on, Ryn," Lucas said, and Brayden and I went toward the laptop together.

Hesitantly, I focused on the screen. There was my apartment door, the living room, my bedroom and my art studio all showing at once. There was nothing and then…me, coming into the art studio. Grant pressed fast forward and I saw myself painting Lucas, then moving to the chair. I watched myself fall asleep and then pop up, just the way I'd woken up.

No surprises but… "What am I doing?" I asked out loud, stared closer at the screen. Because I wasn't standing there waking up. I was moving, toward the paintings. Picking up the paintbrush, then putting it down, and I hadn't done that when I'd woken up.

I was standing in front of the paintings then, and they were in the order I'd remembered leaving them in.

At least they were, until I started moving them around.

I was sleepwalking…and I was moving the paintings around.

Moving them. Staring at them. Reordering them. Standing back and gazing at them, shaking my head as if trying to make sense of them.

I was the intruder. I was the one breaking into my own life, trying to break into my past and break it open…

I was the intruder in my own life.

"You want your memories," Lucas murmured when I'd calmed down somewhat. It took several shots of whiskey to get me to this point, and I was curled on the couch, blankets around me, with the promise that Grant would return with food soon.

"I'm not taking those pills."

Lucas didn't say anything, but I knew what he was thinking. I also didn't think I'd been moving my own paintings.

"You should take the pills away from me. Take them to your place."

"Suppose you need them?"

"Fine. Sleep here while I work. Pocket the pills—or take the pills up to Brayden's."

"You've got nothing to prove to me. If you need the pills—"

"I don't."

"You take them," he finished. "You've done nothing wrong. Your memories need to come out. They're trying to tell you something. So listen."

"I feel like I'm going crazy. Like something inside me is trying to take over, and it's winning."

Lucas's eyes clouded after I shared that. "You're not crazy."

"You don't know me, Lucas, because I don't even know myself," I challenged. "What if I escaped a mental institution? Or prison? What if I'm a murderer and I've had surgery to avoid detection?"

"Like in 'Face Off'?"

"This isn't funny."

"No, it's not. Because I do know *you*, Ryn. I know you jump in to help your friends, that you can kick ass, so there's bite behind your bark. I know that you lose yourself in your work and you could never be with someone who doesn't get that or accept it. I know how to make you come, hard and fast and slow and easy. I know your body better than you."

I blinked at him, because he seemed to know more about me than I did. And then I held the pill bottle to him. "There should be a full bottle. I haven't been taking them at all."

Lucas took the bottle from me and opened it. I expected to see more pills pour out than what sat in his palm.

I practically whispered. "You have to believe me."

"I do," he said shortly. "But you've got an enemy."

One that was determined to drive me over the edge. I turned from Lucas and the pills and back to my paintings. "The flowers…Lucas, I didn't buy myself the daffodils. I know I didn't."

His expression hardened. "You haven't gotten any since we put the alarms in place, right?"

"Right."

"I hate to say this, but if you were bringing in the flowers yourself, you'd still be doing it."

"So someone was coming in here with the flowers," I said in a whisper. I wasn't sure if I should feel better or worse about that, but at least I knew I wasn't totally crazy. "I wasn't making it up. I swear—it happened."

"I don't think you were."

But then it sunk in. "What if I was sleepwalking? What if I thought other flowers were daffodils when I was in one of my fugue states?" I hated the way he looked at me, sympathy and worry. "I have to find out what's in my past. I have to, no matter the cost."

He blew out a breath that hissed between his teeth. "Did you ever stop to consider that it might be better for you to never remember your past?"

I answered without hesitation. "Every day of my life."

17

A WEEK LATER, I met with Gabrielle for lunch at her apartment. Her interview teasers were beginning to leak and I couldn't go online without seeing a mention of the movie or of her. We'd texted daily since our lunch but this was my first time seeing her.

Since he knew that Gabrielle had shared her past with me, Lucas didn't seem worried about me seeing her, and neither did Brayden or Grant, so in my mind she was cleared. Surely none of those men would allow me to get close to a threat.

I'd let my guard down with her, maybe too fast, but she'd been in the right place at the right time. She'd read me, and anyone else might've taken advantage of my vulnerable position at Jared's book party. But she'd been in one too, with a career burgeoning like a swelling wave, and we clung to each other and our respective secrets. Next to Brayden, Lucas and Grant, Gabrielle was the first outsider—and the first female—in my life I'd ever considered a good friend. Susan was my mother figure, but beyond her, I'd always shied away from women.

Meghan was probably the best example of why.

"Hey, thanks for sneaking in to see me!" Gabrielle threw her arms around me when I entered her apartment. I'd gone through the garage to avoid the paps that had been stalking her since the news of her part in the movie broke. Thankfully, I was still able to stalk around mostly unnoticed, especially away from the gallery world.

Gabrielle could've used me for publicity. Then again, I could've used her too.

"No problem," I told her as I hugged her back then unbundled myself, taking my hoodie and cap off. She'd set up a beautiful meal by a picture window with the gorgeous view of the park she had. "Are you okay?"

"I'm not planning on googling myself ever again, but I think I'm okay. I'm already booked on a million shows for the week the interview comes out, so I'll let you know then. I might need to hide out at your place for a while."

"Just let me know."

"Come sit and eat."

I noticed that the elegant trays of food were all comfort foods—dumplings and potatoes and empanadas. An 'appetizer is the main meal' kind of party. Plus chocolate cake. "This looks delicious."

"I know." Gabrielle smiled and began to fill her plate as I settled in across from her and did the same. "I'm not eating carbs this week, so you're not seeing this." Then she gave me a semi-devious look. "Want to see the script?"

"Ugh. I've seen enough of Jared's work to last me a lifetime."

"True." She pointed the fork in my direction before spearing another dumpling. "He doesn't know we're hanging out. But he never talks to us. Any directions? He whispers to the director. Then the director tells us, like we don't know where it's coming from. It helps that the guy playing Jared is way less douchey than Jared actually is. No offense."

"Zero taken. Are you and said co-star getting cozy?"

"There's chemistry, but he's very married. I won't fuck with that. Damned Midwestern values." She took a sip of wine. "Any new developments?"

I shrugged. "It's all so messed up. Jared is still bugging Brayden about using my paintings in the movie. He refuses to take no for an answer. Made

Brayden promise to convince me."

Her brows rose. "Um, that's crazy that he won't just stop."

"That was my first reaction. But…" I told her Brayden's theory. She downed the last half of her glass of wine in one gulp. "I guess you don't agree."

"I just want Jared to leave you alone. That fucker." She filled her wine glass. "No more after this for me, okay?"

"I have no shoot to get up for."

"Young ingénues can't have circles," she said. I saw no evidence of any such circles on Gabrielle's face and she wasn't wearing much makeup either. She just looked relaxed. "Have you been working a ton?"

"Trying to." I took a second helping. I hadn't wanted to mention the part about my paintings being moved…or that I'd been sleepwalking. Not until I understood it all better myself.

"You said that you know Jared made up your past, right?" Gabrielle said suddenly. "I guess what he imagines it to be. But the thing is…how would either of us know if that were true or not?"

We wouldn't. It was my turn to gulp the wine. "Is that why I never heard from him again?"

"The way he talks about you in the book? Like you're the one love of his life who got away."

I rolled my eyes. "And thank God for that."

THE INTERVIEW JARED GAVE to Ann Maslow was everything I'd expected it to be. Brayden had already read it when he handed it over, and I could tell by the look on his face that he was pissed off.

Lucas and Grant were there too, I guessed for moral support.

"I knew she'd pull this," I muttered as I skimmed some of his answers regarding her seeing me and Jared together at his book party.

Ann: It seems like you know Ryn Taylor well. Is there history there?

Jared: I love her paintings.

Ann: How long have you loved her paintings for?

Jared: Long enough.

"He's the one not denying he knew you before—at least not very hard," Brayden pointed out. "She's doing her job, just a little too damned well. And, to add insult to injury, Jared called again—this morning—about the paintings. I told him you hadn't made a decision yet, and it's all I can do not to tell him to fuck off."

"He knows I'm looking for my past. If it comes out during this timeframe…" I trailed off.

"Yeah, your life will make for great publicity for him." Brayden rolled his eyes. "He's pushing you, Ryn. He doesn't care about putting you in danger or making you lose it over all of this."

I didn't point out the obvious, that I'd put myself in danger all by my lonesome just fine.

"Breathe, Ryn," Lucas said, a hand on my shoulder.

"I am. And I can't let Jared keep playing these mind games with me," I announced. "I have to confront him." When Lucas and Brayden both looked less than thrilled with that idea, I persisted with, "Jared knew I'd be in the city. He knew I was having my show."

"He moved his party," Grant broke in. "It was supposed to be the week before your show. It was moved two weeks before."

"How do you know that?" I asked.

"There was a call from his camp to Brayden's gallery right before the change of venue. Maybe two minutes in between the calls," Grant confirmed. "The party was booked for a restaurant but they couldn't accommodate the last-minute change that Jared insisted on."

Lucas swore under his breath.

"He hasn't told anyone who I am," I said finally.

"Not at the party, no. But since he saw you, with each subsequent interview, he's hinting," Grant told me. "Maybe I'm just reading into it, but I don't want to take that chance. You should call him."

"No," Brayden said loudly.

"Ryn, I think you should make a date to go out with him. Try to figure out his end game. See if he's using the fact that he can reveal you to leverage something else," Grant explained, shooting an impatient glance at Lucas.

"I can definitely get him to reveal his plan," Lucas announced, his tone fierce and his hands fisted.

"Yes, that will go over really well," I told Lucas.

"You're not going out alone with him," he shot back.

"Why not? It wouldn't be a date."

"Maybe not to you."

"Oh, come on," I scoffed. "I meant nothing

to him. He used me for book fodder." I noticed Brayden shaking his head. "What? You told me that's all it was," I said.

"I got the feeling he's still very into you."

"He's pretending to be, then—it's part of his game. Grant's right—I've got to find all of this out from Jared before it goes any further." I grabbed Jared's card from Grant's hand. "I'm calling him now. Once he reveals that I'm the basis for his book, I've got no place left to hide."

And even though in many ways that might be a relief, after the park incident, the thought scared the hell out of me.

Before I could back out—or Lucas could stop me—I went into another room with my cell phone, locked the door and dialed. "Hey Jared, it's Ryn."

"I knew you'd call." It was said without smugness, but he definitely sounded pleased.

I closed my eyes and forced myself to remember that I was trying to out-manipulate him. "Listen," I started before he could say something else that would make Lucas crazy, since I realized he'd picked the lock and was listening in on the conversation over my shoulder. "I was wondering if we could meet for a drink."

"Sure. I've got time tonight before I leave for the west coast." He named a place that was close to Brayden's gallery before adding, "How about I pick you up? I'm guessing you live close by."

"How about I…" Lucas growled.

"I'll meet you there. Six o'clock," I said hurriedly, then practically hung up on his, "I can't wait to see you."

"I'm going with you," Lucas said firmly.

"That would go over really well." I put a hand on his chest. "It's important for me to do this alone."

"It's important to me to keep you safe. No question—I'll be there. In the bar."

I sighed. It was the best I was going to get, and besides, he was right. It wasn't just Jared I needed to worry about. If anything, Jared was the easier force than my past threatened to be. "As long as you're with Grant. Because he can control you."

"When it comes to you, no one can control me." He meant it.

"I know you're worried. I get it. And I love you for it." I wrapped myself around him.

"You love me for it? Or you just love me?" he asked seriously.

"Both," I answered, just as seriously. I got a smile in return, one that relaxed his expression and took the haunted look from his eyes.

That evening, Jared was already at the bar, waiting in casual but expensive clothes. Because he wore them well, he was attracting a good deal of female attention. I could understand that for sure, but now that I knew him his handsomeness was lost on me.

"Ryn, hey." He stood, kissed me on both cheeks and then gave me a hug. I tried not to shrink away from any of it and managed what I hoped was a sincere smile when he pulled back. I don't think he'd notice either way. He wasn't aware of other people's emotions, just how he could manipulate them overall.

"Thanks for making time for me so quickly." I slid onto a stool he'd pulled out for me and he took his seat again. We ordered, a martini for him, a margarita for me, and made small talk about his upcoming tour while we waited for them.

"They've got me booked up. Between the book tour and the movie, I'm spinning." He didn't look unhappy about that at all.

"The book's doing well, then?" I managed.

"It's a commercial and critical success," he couldn't help but boast.

"How wonderful for you." God, I couldn't have held back the sarcasm if I'd tried, and it was flying over Jared's head anyway. Nothing could've penetrated his high. He was oblivious to anything but his success that appeared to be mounting as we spoke.

The whole thing made my skin crawl. And here I'd thought critics were the only parasites I'd needed to worry about.

"So," he asked, after we'd made a toast to old times (and I swore I heard Lucas groan from across the bar where he and Grant were waiting), "I'm guessing you read the book."

"I...couldn't," I lied. "It's too hard."

He sat back, properly chastened...or pretending to be. "Everything's fair game for me. I can't help it. But I'd never do anything that would hurt you."

Too late. "You're wanting to use my paintings in your movie. You've mentioned that in a major magazine interview. You're coy when reporters ask if we know each other. I'm just worried that you'll mention me. Now that my name's a little more out there..."

"A little more? Ryn, the buzz *you're* getting is tremendous. I'd think you'd be more worried about that than anything."

"Wait, are you saying if someone from my past finds me, that it'll be my fault? Because that's kind of a dick thing to say."

He put his hands up. "You always did have a temper."

And the gloves were off. I pointed at him. "Don't you act like you know me. You don't—and you never cared to."

He leaned forward, pushing my hand down. "And you still shared your life with me."

"I didn't think you'd put it in a book." We'd managed to keep our voices low enough, but if anyone was looking at us, it was obvious we weren't having the most pleasant of conversations.

Jared shrugged. "You didn't tell me not to."

"I didn't think I needed a nondisclosure agreement to fuck you."

He shook his head. "Ryn, when we spent that time together, I wasn't ready for anything serious. I'm in a different place now. And you obviously don't care about your past catching up to you. I never figured any of this would be an issue. If you're going to cash in on it, then it's fair game for me to do so as well. We're just two creatives, helping each other."

"You can't be this stupid."

He flinched. "The book's a peace offering. And since you seem to want to find out who you really are, I want to help you. You started this by showing your paintings, granting interviews and coming to New York. If your name comes out, because of that or because of my book, someone from your past can come forward and claim you.

I'm assuming that's exactly what you want."

"Don't you dare tell me what I want." My voice held a fury that startled him. "I don't need your help with this. You've done enough."

"We make a good story. Think about it. We could be good together, Ryn. We *were* good together."

"Funny that you believe that now."

"I was young. I know I hurt you but I didn't meant to."

"You can't expect that I'd date you now. You're trying to convince me to come out for extra publicity for *you*."

He studied me. "I think you'd be a great asset. I'd love to consult with you on the script."

"Go fuck yourself." My hand gripped my drink, and I barely suppressed the urge to throw it in his face. Instead, I walked out.

And he followed, gripped my elbow before I got to the door to leave. "What did you expect? Do you think you could do all this and keep your life exactly the same? Because if you did, you're completely delusional."

I pulled away from him. "You think I wanted all this attention?"

"I don't see why else you'd do this, Ryn. You always were starved for attention."

His words stung. Maybe they'd been partially

true at one point, but certainly now it seemed like he was building his case against me. "Maybe I was. I liked you. A lot. And what I told you was private."

He shook his head. "Like you pointed out, I didn't need a nondisclosure agreement to fuck you."

I gaped at him, but before I could actually react further, Jared was torn from next to me and Lucas was basically dragging him out the door of the bar. I followed in time to watch Lucas punch Jared in his perfect cheekbone—twice—then continue to kick the shit out of him…at least until Grant pulled Lucas off.

Flashbulbs popped. I lowered my head and tried to disappear. Grant helped with that immediately, spiriting me away inside the waiting car, leaving Lucas to lunge at Jared again.

I watched through the dark window from inside the car. Jared was stunned, pointing at Lucas from his position on the ground, yelling, "I'll fucking sue you. And her."

Lucas lunged at Jared again but he didn't get very far before Grant caught him. Jared was scuttling backward on the concrete until he finally ended up being dragged from the pavement by what looked like a friend and into a waiting town car.

Of course, the paparazzi continued snapping pictures and shooting their video until Lucas and Grant got into the car with me. Grant, in the driver's seat and Lucas in the back with me.

As Grant maneuvered the car into the heavy traffic, none of us spoke. I was holding my breath until Grant found a break in the traffic and sped away.

Grant pulled in front of my building and Lucas and I got out. "I'll call you," Lucas told Grant.

"Way to keep it under wraps," Grant said.

"Fuck that. We can protect her. Let her goddamn past come for her. I'm not going to let her be held hostage anymore."

"I hear you, brother."

Lucas nodded, then shut the door. We went into the building, into the elevator and finally we were alone in my apartment. Lucas was still vibrating with a palpable anger.

I put my hands on his cheeks. "It's okay, Lucas. I'm okay."

Lucas growled, "I'll fucking kill him for doing that to you. It's not okay. But it will be."

His expression was stony and I didn't bother to argue. He scared the hell out of me, and I liked it. A lot. And he knew it, pulled me to him harder, held me tighter. He growled. Nipped my neck and I felt the wildness rise in him. It would push out of him, invade me the way he would when he took me. And I wanted to take that ride with him. Let him push me harder and higher, until I was breathing him, controlled by him fully.

"Yes," I whispered.

"You don't fully believe me." He popped buttons off my shirt, opening it bit by bit, slid it off my shoulders. "But you will."

"I know you were right—about Jared. About what he was doing," I murmured.

"I'm going to fuck you, and you're going to keep saying that to me. Over and over." Lucas swept me up and carried me into the bedroom.

After he put me down on the bed, he reached into his pocket and pulled out my knife that he must've taken from my bag. "I love that you carry this. Love even more that I bet you know how to use it to protect yourself."

I did. I wasn't sure how, but I knew I could protect myself...or at least die trying. I felt like I was living proof of that.

He lay the blade flat against my skin along my sternum. It was so cold, or maybe my skin was so hot—fever hot. I shuddered lightly, then held my breath as he slid the knife upward, then flicked it up casually. It sliced through my bra at the same time his fingers circled my clit, the tight bundle of nerves giving in easily to the relief of tension.

He never broke contact, his eyes boring into me as I shuddered and came against his fingers. The knife lay against my sternum the whole time.

And then he was naked, the knife gone, and he was seated fully inside me. I wrapped around him, still floating but wanting more.

"Greedy," he murmured.

"You made me that way."

"Good." He was throbbing inside me, so ready to come but holding off. For me. "I've been touching you in my head all night. Watching you on that stool with him…driving me crazy. I wanted to be between your legs. Licking you. Making you scream."

A delicious blast of heat shoots straight through to my core. His palms are on either side of me, his biceps a ripple of ink and muscle. And then he's devouring me.

Then again, I'm devouring him too, so fair is fair.

My body winds tighter and tighter until I'm sure I can't take anymore

But I can. I do.

19

"GOT TO GO," LUCAS murmured early the next morning.

"Where?" I wrapped a hand around his wrist in protest as he slid out of bed, trying to keep the connection with him even as he stood.

"Police station."

Immediately, I was up out of the bed and next to him. "What? Why?"

He pulled his jeans on and met my gaze head-on. "I'm wanted for questioning."

"Jared called the police?"

"Yes."

"He's saying you assaulted him? Are you turning yourself in?" I was gathering my clothes, prepared to go with Lucas to the station.

"Yes. And yes." He took me by the shoulders and stopped my frantic getting-dressed motions.

"Please, stay here. It's better all around if you do. I can handle this, okay? Trust me."

I did. "I do."

"Good." He brushed his knuckles over my cheek. "After I talk to the police and my lawyer, I'll call you."

I wasn't sure how I knew he was lying about that last part, but I knew he was just the same.

That afternoon, the pictures concerning my date gone wrong with Jared appeared everywhere and anywhere, both in print and online. And someone had left a paper at my door so I wouldn't miss it. It'd been folded over to the picture and I wouldn't open the door, just in case. Brayden came down and brought it in when I called him about it.

He grimaced as he looked at it and then handed it to me. The first shot was me exiting, and then Jared following. And then Lucas and Jared fighting.

"This isn't good," I muttered. It had to be Dan Turner who'd left me that paper—I had no doubt about it. "Did Jared call the paparazzi there? Did he want these taken?"

Brayden shrugged. "It fits his publicity-hungry

M.O."

My intercom buzzed and Brayden answered it. The doorman informed us that there was a police officer who needed to speak with us.

Brayden and I stared at each other after he'd agreed that the officer could come up, and we didn't speak a word until the knock at the door.

"Listen more than you speak," Brayden reminded me before opening the door and letting the man, who introduced himself as Detective Parker, in.

"You're Ryn Taylor?" Parker asked and I nodded. "And you're Brayden Hamilton?"

"Yes," Brayden said.

"I want to inform you both that Jared Connor is missing."

"Missing?" I echoed.

"What does she need to know that for?" Brayden demanded.

Parker eyed him calmly. "Because she was one of the last people seen with him, along with her boyfriend, Lucas Caine."

"He left the restaurant with someone—a friend or a driver, but he wasn't alone," I reminded the officer.

"Yes, he did. The employee drove Jared home. Jared called the police, gave a report by phone. He was supposed to meet with me this afternoon, and when he didn't show up we went to his apartment. Around the same time, his assistant called us to tell us that Jared hadn't shown for an important work event this morning."

"This is all fascinating," Brayden broke in, and I wondered what happened to the whole 'listen more and talk less' advice. "But this has nothing to do with us. We're not Jared's keepers."

"It has everything to do with Miss Taylor, as she was seen in an altercation with him," Parker pointed out.

"I didn't touch him," I protested.

"You fought with Mr. Connor and then your boyfriend punched him," Parker said.

"Maybe he ran off to lick his wounds," Brayden muttered.

"His agent said there's no way he'd miss a spot on a big morning news show."

"I thought you couldn't file a missing person's report until after twenty-four hours had passed," Brayden asked.

"In this case, I'm making an exception."

I frowned. "I honestly have no idea where he'd be. I don't know him that well. Wait, he said he was fitting in the drink with me because he was leaving for the west coast late last night."

"He lied," Parker said flatly. But why would Jared lie about something so innocuous?

Just then, Grant appeared. His feet were bare and he wore sweats and a T-shirt, like he'd come over from another apartment. Except he didn't live in this building.

He walked in, saying, "Sorry to interrupt. I'm looking for Brayden."

Parker stared at him and then at Brayden. "How well do you know Grant Loughlin?"

"Well enough," Brayden said easily. Grant moved closer to him, casually leaning an elbow on the countertop next to him.

"Where were you last night between nine and midnight?" Parker demanded of Brayden.

"He was with me," Grant replied. After half a second, Brayden nodded.

Parker's eyes narrowed, not in a disgusted way. "Bullshit. You're alibiing each other."

Grant caught an easy hand around the back of Brayden's neck and pulled him in for a kiss. And for the love of God, that set my heart on fire, because if this was their first kiss, it reached implode levels immediately.

"Just because you're hot for each other doesn't mean I believe you," Parker told them as they pulled apart. "You'd better hope I don't find a trace of either of you on the security camera footage I'm pulling from the surrounding buildings today."

"You won't," Grant said with a smile. He hadn't

let go of Brayden's neck, let his thumb trace the fading hickeys with intent. Brayden looked sufficiently stunned and more than a little shaken. Grant just looked pleased with himself.

Parker turned his stony gaze on me. "We'll be in touch, Miss Taylor."

I didn't doubt it, but I held my tongue until he left the apartment. I shut and locked the door behind him and watched him, through the peephole, go down the hall.

When I turned back to Brayden and Grant, I noted that Brayden had put as much space as he could between him and Grant, all while trying to appear not-freaked out about their kiss.

"How did you know he was here?" I asked Grant.

"He came to Lucas's looking for me," Grant explained. "I figured he'd come here next. You already had the hickeys and I needed an alibi."

"Next time, find a different one," Brayden muttered.

"You needed one too," Grant reminded him. "You both do."

And I had Lucas as mine, which was probably the least helpful alibi ever at this point. "Where's Lucas?"

"He had to go out of town for a bit," Grant said cryptically, and my heart sank.

20

TWO DAYS PASSED, WITH no word from Lucas. I remained holed up, not reading about myself online. Brayden and Grant promised they'd keep me up to date on the Jared situation, but as of that evening, no one had heard from him either.

"He's probably doing it to draw more attention to his movie," Brayden had surmised. "Either that or he's trying to screw Lucas."

Which meant Jared would be screwing me as well.

But all the waiting was getting me antsy. I'd gotten wind of a gallery showing of up-and-coming artists. I was one myself but I'd had far more advantages than most new artists, and Brayden agreed with me that it would be good to lend a show of support by going. Brayden was able to snag two last-minute tickets from a fellow gallery owner who wasn't able to go.

Gabrielle called me right as we were getting ready to walk in. "Two minutes," I told Brayden and when he moved to talk to some industry people he knew on the improvised red carpet, I slid into the background and answered the phone.

"You're all over the papers," Gabrielle said by way of greeting. "TMZ too."

"I thought you didn't read that."

"I do when it's not about me." She lowered her voice. "Jared's not on set. It's the first day he's missed since filming's started." That was a punch in the gut, but she didn't seem as concerned about it as the police were. "The director's thrilled. Frankly, so am I. Maybe you can ask Lucas to beat Jared up more often so he's got to stay home and lick his wounds."

"Anything for you," I joked, even though my stomach soured a little. I wanted to believe that about Jared, that he was embarrassed and hiding or plotting and hiding, but the fact that the police were involved...the fact that Lucas left town...

For work, I reminded myself.

We spoke for a few seconds more and then I hung up and joined Brayden to go inside, without mentioning what Gabrielle had told me. Brayden needed a break as much as I did. And even though people here would know about what happened, tonight also wasn't focused on me. Most people seemed to respect that.

I was sure the photographers wouldn't, which was why we'd avoided them and went in through a side door.

The event's venue was a full hotel ballroom and it was packed. There was a showcase of artists and the program explained that there would be scholarships and grants awarded that evening from several artist's foundations.

Most of those artists were deceased. One of them caught my eye. His name was Bane, and he'd died tragically, much too young. He became famous post-death, so much so that his art was worth millions. He'd been a big, blazing talent with a reputation for being crazy. He'd been well before my time, coming onto my radar not long after my hospitalization.

He'd died around that time and I studied his works for inspiration. I'd heard of Bane in that mythical way that young talent burns bright. Ultimately, it's unsustainable. Rumors said Bane was troubled. *Crazy*, some said, but I knew how easy it was to mistake extreme creativity for crazy.

Then again, I also knew they could be two sides of the same coin.

Brayden nudged me. "What're you thinking

about over there?"

"Where's Zack tonight?" I asked brightly.

"No clue," Brayden said with a tight smile. His hickeys had faded to almost nothing, but it'd been obvious how much they'd annoyed Grant. I was intrigued, but knew better than to ask about that part of it.

Instead, I pressed, "Do you want to have a clue?" as he sipped his Jack and Coke.

After a long moment, he replied with a simple, "Zack's good for me."

"And the problem is…?"

"I've never liked what's good for me."

I shook my head. "You seem to like it. Him."

His grin was lopsided. "There's the part I like, yeah. But the stuff that comes with it? No."

"The relationship part?"

"Yes. That's a drag. The 'tell me your life and I'll tell you mine.' We'll fuck each other up because of it. He'll try to change me. What was once cool becomes annoying. I don't want that."

Neither did I, so I couldn't blame him. "What if it doesn't have to be like that?"

"Always is."

I know he didn't want to say it would happen to me and Lucas. It wouldn't. Lucas wasn't Jared. Lucas wasn't like any man I'd ever met. He was too strong, too smart to bring that kind of shit into our relationship.

And when I told Brayden all that, all he said was, "So it's a relationship now?"

"Like you didn't know."

He sat back. "From the second you two met, babe."

He sounded a little sad though. I wanted so badly to reassure him, tell him that Lucas and I were fine. Better than fine—amazing, even—and that everything would work out. My past wouldn't hurt me.

Because how could a past hurt me? Past was past, right? "I'm going to browse some paintings before the speakers start."

"Go for it—I'm going to mingle and talk you up."

I shook my head at his smile, knowing he absolutely meant it. And after several minutes and some beautiful artwork, I came upon a piece that grabbed me by the throat, shook me and then dropped me to the ground when it was sure I'd seen what I was supposed to see.

It was a piece tucked into the corner—maybe not Bane's most famous work, one I'd never actually seen before anywhere.

I'd remember it if I had.

I never believed in coincidences, but my life to this point had been all about looking for signs, for anything that would point me in the right direction.

I'd convinced myself that I was so obsessed with my past that I was the one making more out of it than was there. That if I simply stopped, I'd learn the truth, and that truth would be "everything's fine and the past is gone."

Dust.

Dawn.

Both were represented in Bane's piece, a moody, dirty, just before the sunrise painting. A tribute to Aerosmith's song and I got chills looking at what hung in front of me.

The past wasn't past. It was right here, slapping me in the face, planning on taking my future and strangling it between its guiding, all-knowing hands.

The name of his piece? *Past is always Present*.

"It's not over." I said it to myself, out loud. My words were lost, snapped up by the noise of the crowds, the melee surrounding my dawning understanding of the situation.

The past was *never* past.

I had to give it to Bane—he'd known so much more than I ever had. Maybe he'd died because of it.

I was still reeling from the truth in the work of a man I'd never meet when the squeal of microphone feedback startled me back into the present.

Then the speaker started his introductions and after a minute the room was quiet. "Thank you all for coming tonight to celebrate the hottest up-and-coming artists. Tonight, we have a special guest who will award the first of several grants in honor of an artist we lost far too soon. Please welcome Grant Loughlin."

Lucas's Grant.

Brayden looked like he'd seen a ghost. He was staring at Grant as if seeing him for the first time. I looked between them as Grant approached the podium.

It was only then I noticed Lucas in the crowd. His gaze locked on mine, but then Grant began to speak, and his words most definitely caught my attention.

"I'm here tonight in honor of the artist you all know as Bane. He was an immense talent. A generous artist, as evidenced by those who knew him best. I'm one of those who did, because Bane was my brother," he began, and next to me I heard Brayden's sharp intake of breath, followed by a muttered, "Fuck me."

I was confused as to why Brayden would be so upset about Grant's connection to Bane. He'd never mentioned Bane in any context other than the man's status as a famous artist.

Grant looked broken as he spoke, eloquently, about the loss of his brother and ended with, "I'm honored to be able to help young artists in Bane's name," before announcing the three young artists who would be awarded money to further their creative endeavors.

There was much applause and picture taking. Grant ducked his head for most of it. I noticed because I'd seen him do it before, as if he didn't want to have his picture taken at all.

I turned to where Brayden had been standing next to me, but he was gone.

In his place stood Dan Turner. "I didn't realize you were such a big supporter of the arts," I managed.

"Helps me when it comes time for the insurance investigations," he countered, then lifted a glass of what appeared to be water in my direction—a mock toast. "You're a smart girl, Ryn. Are you putting the pieces together yet?"

I'm not a girl, I wanted to tell him, but the connections were like misfiring neurons and making it impossible to think in a straight line.

Grant. Bane.

Lucas.

Brayden.

And Dan Turner. "I want you to stop taunting

me and tell me what you know. More than that, I need you to prove it…or leave me alone."

"I don't think you can handle it."

"Maybe not, but I'm not sure how that's any of your concern. You seem intent on my knowing this stuff, but I'm tired. And I'm prepared to report you and get a restraining order on you."

"I'll get you your proof. In the meantime, ask Brayden to fill in some pieces. He knows a lot of them." He leaned in. "Ask him how Bane died."

I narrowed my eyes, but before I could respond further, he was gone. I'll admit, I wasn't sure what I'd just demanded of him—it could be what threw my anxiety over the edge.

I went to look for Brayden to do just that, my brain reeling from information overload, and ran into Lucas instead, who was engrossed at looking at one of Bane's largest-scale paintings. I knew he saw me, so I stood next to him, stared at his profile and waited a few moments before asking, "What are you doing here?" I asked.

"Supporting a friend," he replied without turning to look at me.

I looked away from him and joined his staring at the large, rough canvas, a brilliant wash of colors. On first glance it might look as though there was just maniacal paint slashes but no, emerging from underneath the vicious color was a beautiful sunrise. Night was over but morning light was coming fast. He'd held onto that, and I couldn't help but choke up thinking that he'd held onto himself, night after night, until one night, he couldn't. Whether it seemed like it was too long or he'd gotten upset with someone or his art wasn't coming out as he'd planned…he didn't fight. Not the way he had here.

"He was wrestling with some major demons." Lucas stood behind me, staring at the painting.

"Do you recognize them?"

I saw a small tic in his jaw before he simply glanced between me and the painting. "I can recognize a demon from forty yards."

He wasn't kidding.

I turned back to the painting, and it was only then I realized I was staring at a colorized, final version of Lucas's backpiece. His tattoo was gray scale, most likely a smaller-sized original artist's sketch of one of Bane's most famous works, *The Flame*. But before I could ask Lucas questions— questions he no doubt wouldn't answer, Brayden found me.

"Ryn, sorry, I—"

"I'm not in the mood for sorry," I told him, my voice shaking from anger. "How did *you* know Bane?"

"Who in the art world doesn't know him?" was

his vague, bullshit answer.

"Fuck you," came out of my mouth next, and he paled.

"Ryn—"

"No. No more 'Ryn, it's for your own good' speeches. You're all hiding things from me." I looked between Lucas and Brayden. "Maybe it's the same things or maybe different things…but somehow they're all going to connect. I feel it. And I've got enough shit to deal with in my own life."

A hand closed over my shoulder. Grant. His eyes held the same haunted look I'd seen both Brayden and Lucas wear at times when he told me, "This isn't the time or place."

"It never is with you guys," I muttered, but I let him steer me away from Brayden and out the door. Once outside, he loosened his hold but remained on alert for whatever unknown dangers lurked.

"In there." He pointed to a coffee shop a few doors down and we walked to it quickly. It was relatively empty, and we took a seat in the back. He ordered up coffee and pie for both of us. "They've got the best pie here."

I wasn't hungry at all. I shifted, watching him stir the cream into his coffee intently. "Will Lucas be mad I'm here with you?"

He smiled. "Lucas is mad he's not here with

you."

"Are you going to tell me the truth?"

He stared at me with steady amber eyes. "You know my truth. I'm Lucas's best friend and he's mine. I'd do anything for him. Bane was my younger brother, and, despite what anyone says to the contrary, he killed himself by jumping off the roof of a building in Miami when he was twenty-one years old."

That knocked the breath out of me. Grant had spoken in a no-nonsense way, but there was no hiding the pain he felt. "I'm so sorry."

"I was away—still in the military. On deployment on the other side of the world," he explained. I guessed that's where the scar on his neck had come from. Up close, it was more impressive—a badge of honor. I could see the ragged edges and knew I'd have to paint him. "Bane left home when I did. I'd begged him to hold on for another year, until he turned seventeen, so I could save some money. But he wouldn't put all that on me. He said, 'One day I'll be sending you money, because you deserve it.'"

He stopped, took a shuddered breath and I reached out and touched his arm. "You took care of him growing up."

"That's how he saw it. But he took care of me just as much, and just as hard."

A fleeting thought of the possibility that I might have siblings crossed my mind, and I wondered what it would be like to feel that bond, to feel such incredible pain once it was broken. "Who disputes that he killed himself?"

"Turner."

"So Dan Turner's interested in me because of my connection…to you?"

"There's more to it than that, but Bane is a part of it." He sat back. "It's hard to talk about this with an artist, but I know you'll understand the most. Bane was an incredible talent, but there was a darkness there too. If he didn't have it, he wouldn't have been so good, and still, it cost him, every single day of his life. It was always a fight."

I did understand, to a lesser degree, no doubt because of the memory loss—which kept me distracted, and curious enough to stop the complete descent into madness. "It's a hard gift to have," I admitted. "I worry that it will disappear if my memory comes back, but it would be a relief."

Creativity was an intense, brutal taskmaster and it could strip me of everything if I wasn't careful. I don't think Bane was careful. Maybe he couldn't be. Sometimes it was easier to give in to it than to fight it, and I wondered if I'd eventually succumb to that point. "So Lucas and Brayden both knew Bane too?"

"Yes," he confirmed. Maybe Bane's death was responsible for the tension between the two men. Before I could ask, Grant added, "I didn't meet Lucas until after Bane's death. And I met Brayden for the first time, unofficially, when you met Lucas at the gallery."

"And even then, Brayden had no idea you were Bane's brother."

"Brayden didn't know until tonight," Grant confirmed. "Bane used to refer to me by a nickname to them. But I felt like I knew Brayden long before that,

through my brother's letters. He'd write me all the time." His smile was wistful. "I can't tell you the amounts of money I've been offered to publish them, but I never would."

I wanted to read them, because I was always jealous of someone's memories, their ability to recall them. I gathered them, inhaled them as if they could be mine if I tried hard enough. But Bane's would be far too raw and personal. "I'm so sorry—about my reaction. About your brother."

"Your reaction was justified." He motioned for another cup of coffee. "I've been up thinking about that damned speech for two nights. I'm running on fumes."

"I've been there."

"I know." He paused. "Bane was like that. He'd

need to be slipped a sleeping pill when he'd been up for three nights and started painting clowns."

"What's wrong with clowns?"

"He hated them."

I couldn't help but smile, because I'd been there. "For me, it was ponies. Like Rainbow Brite ponies. I called Brayden, convinced I'd come up with the next big thing. He drove to me at three in the morning and made me some special tea. I didn't wake up for days. Hey wait…"

Grant grinned. "He learned that from Lucas—they both used to do it for Bane."

I liked having something in common with Bane, if only to make Grant smile when they talked about him.

"He wasn't like you, Ryn. He wasn't strong."

I was going to argue that I wasn't either, but something stopped me. Maybe because deep down, I knew I'd be lying. "It's a hard gift to balance."

"Always was for him. He was too sensitive. Took everything to heart. I got it—there was no way he could paint like he did and not be, but I also knew there was no way he could stay that sensitive and survive this world." He shook his head. "I offered to buy him a place away from everyone and everything right before I came back home. But it was too late. He'd already let too much of the world in, despite how hard Lucas and Brayden both always tried to shield him from it, and that really fucked with Bane bad."

I'd always wanted to believe it was never too late, but looking into Grant's eyes that night, I had to admit defeat.

21

TURNER WAS WAITING FOR me when the
elevator opened. My apartment was down at the
end of the hall but I didn't want him following me.
I stood in front of him. "Why are you here?"

"You spoke to Grant."

"Yes. He told me how Bane died." I crossed my
arms. "It doesn't sound like there's any way to hide
what happened."

"Right. A suicide's always a suicide."

"He was troubled. Everyone who knew him
said so."

Turner shook his head slowly. "You're really in
deep with these guys. They got you drinking the
Kool-Aid fast and furiously. Are they helping you
find whoever's stalking you?"

I wouldn't share with him that I was
sleepwalking and moving my own paintings.

I wasn't making up the flowers, or the danger. "We're done. Anything further you need to say about the missing paintings can be done through Brayden's attorney."

"What about your family?" he asked. "Or lack thereof?"

"I have family."

"Right—the café owner and her husband who took in a seventeen-year-old foster kid out of the blue. That's not suspicious at all," he commented.

I fisted my hands tightly but resisted showing emotions. I'd been prepared for this, but still I couldn't get the damned words to come out of my mouth. He didn't look all that surprised and that's what got me talking. "You've done some digging on me, before I got involved with Lucas. Why was that necessary?"

"Because before the age of eighteen, your story reads like a couple of US Marshals decided to get creative. I can't ask if you're in witness protection and you can't answer…"

"I'm not."

"None of this is good, Miss *Taylor*." He stared at me. "Do you have any idea how Lucas makes his money?"

"I'm guessing you believe you know what Lucas does for a living." I crossed my arms. "What makes you think I don't?"

Turner narrowed his eyes, trying his best to be a human lie detector. He didn't realize that, most of the time, I was impenetrable. "He's told you he's in security. You believe him. And you're playing a really dangerous game. You're way out of your depth here."

"I'm just fine. Thanks for your concern." I went to move past him but he stopped me with his next words.

"Jared Connor is still missing."

I blinked and absorbed that information. "That's not my problem."

"It very much is. Have you considered what I told you about Lucas Caine? That he's a dangerous man? If you have, take it a step further, because who better to draw you in than the man who's stalking you."

The idea of that was horrifying, but I couldn't deny that Turner could be right. Not because I believed Lucas was capable of it, but because of my memory loss.

I didn't say anything though, but Turner continued, "Every time it happens, it pushes you closer to him."

Finally, I broke. "For what purpose? What gain?"

"He becomes obsessed with artists."

I was as obsessed with Lucas as he was with me,

but I didn't know Lucas's relationship with Bane, not well enough to find truth in Turner's words. I wanted to tell him so but I refused to belabor his point. "Go. Now."

Turner began to comply, but not before pulling a folded manila envelope from inside his jacket. He handed it to me. "Read this if you want more truths. Otherwise, enjoy the Kool-Aid. You're not the first and you won't be the last."

I wasn't surprised that Lucas was waiting for me inside my apartment. He opened the door when I was about to put my keys in the lock. "Turner's gone?"

I glanced down the empty hallway. "Appears to be. Am I allowed inside my own place?"

Lucas moved aside, his expression troubled. He shut the door after me and I dropped my bag, kicked off my shoes and turned to face him the way I would a battle. Because that's what this all was, what my life had been for literally as long as I could remember.

Memory was a funny thing, a picture blurred at the edges, a fuzzy snapshot that flashed by too quickly to capture, never mind process.

At least that's how it was for me…like a dream.

All my memories were like dreams—I was never sure what was real or what wasn't. Most of the time it didn't bother me…but nights like tonight, it was all I could think about.

"You moved your paintings again," he said.

"Really? That's what you want to lead with?"

He stood there like a wall in front of me, big and tall and strong and told me, "You need to go. Leave New York before this work consumes you."

"What are you talking about?"

"You're sleepwalking."

"Trying to find my memories," I pointed out. "You know that."

"Someone's trying to push them out of you. And that someone might not have your best interests in mind," he reminded me.

"It doesn't matter. I can't go on like this."

"Yes, you can. You can keep doing your art and forget the things you might be better off not knowing," he said, and I blinked, because Lucas, of all people, knew how much I wanted—needed—those memories. I'd given up the idea of safety to do it, and in my mind, there was no turning back.

"I'm not leaving."

"You're letting this drive you crazy."

"I'm not Bane."

"No," he agreed with a wince. "But you're just as tortured."

It was my turn to wince. "How did he die?"

Lucas blanched. "He killed himself. Threw himself off a building in Florida before I could stop him."

God, his voice sounded so raw and troubled. "You can't…you're not responsible. You know you can't blame yourself."

"You can say it as many times as you'd like, but getting me to believe it?" He shook his head, looked at the ceiling and snorted a laugh with zero humor behind it. "Paint, Ryn. Live a quiet life. Sell your work but don't be a part of this scene."

"Your back. The tattoo…"

"He drew it on me. The day before he killed himself. Told me, 'It's you, man. The flame, looking for its fire.' He was like that. Impulsive. One minute you were talking to him and the next he was drawing on the closest available thing he could find."

"Your bare back was the closest thing?"

"We were on the roof, getting some sun. We lived in a warehouse, top floor. One of the perks."

"You lived with him?"

He nodded. "Three of us. Me, Bane. And Brayden."

The breath caught in my throat. I would deal with Brayden later. "And the tattoo?"

"After he died, I drank a bottle of scotch. Or

three. And I went and had a tattoo artist make the backpiece permanent. Before the ink faded. And Bane, the night he died, he'd worked on the actual piece all night long. Finished it. And then he jumped." His last word was practically a growl.

Turner's words rang in my ears: *He becomes obsessed with artists.* "Did you pose for Bane?"

Lucas frowned. "Not like you're talking about. Not like I did with you. It was different with Bane. Everything was just different."

He looked pained. I wanted to let him off the hook, but I didn't. "How? How was it different?"

"You weren't there, Ryn."

"That's right."

"So let it go."

"I've done that too much. Way too much." After I'd spoken, he stared at me, then shook his head, and got up to leave. "That's your answer? To run?"

"I'm walking, not running."

Are you coming back? That echoed in my mind but I refused to ask it. "You're bad for me."

"Really?" His voice was low, dangerous, and his stare was from a man I almost didn't recognize. "Is that how you feel?"

I couldn't back down now. "Yes."

"Then I won't bother you again." He was gone before I could breathe. Which was good, because that breath ended up being a sob. A deep, ugly one, followed by several more.

Hours later, I pulled myself off the floor, rinsed my face and began to paint. Even though the envelope taunted me the whole time, the urge to create was too strong to fight, and I'd done enough fighting that night.

Only when I'd finished, and the sun started to rise over Manhattan, did I grab the envelope and open it.

Inside was a single sheet of paper, a police report from Miami, Florida circa Bane's death.

His name was listed as Theodore Bane. For a minute, the introduction of Grant Loughlin echoed in my head, but I dismissed it. There were many different reasons—legitimate ones, ones with no suspicious motives—why brothers could have different last names.

It listed survivors as a brother and a father, whereabouts unknown for both. Apparent cause of death was listed as suicide. Motives were given, scrawled words like *depression, manic, drugs*.

Bane had jumped off the building he'd lived in, off the same roof he'd been sitting on with Lucas just hours earlier, just before dawn. He dove off, headfirst from the roof of his own building onto concrete. Five stories high. The coroner concluded that death was instantaneous.

My body reacted, felt the impact of that statement with a deep shudder. I wanted to put the paper down, to believe everything Grant and Lucas had told me. I had no reason not to.

Still, I read farther.

In scrawled writing that was from the cop who'd been on scene, he stated that there was evidence that Bane was pushed, and that the case would be reviewed after the medical examiner inspected the body and the crime scene was gone over thoroughly.

It stated that the police had spoken with Bane a week earlier and he'd made statements that he believed someone was trying to kill him. In Bane's apartment, they'd discovered a note that he'd been supposed to meet with an insurance agent about his art that he'd believed had been stolen.

The insurance man's name was Dan Turner, and he'd confirmed the eight a.m. breakfast meeting that Bane would never attend.

I hadn't realized I'd been holding my breath the entire time I'd been reading that section. I exhaled dizzily and finished with the final note on the page. A lone Post-it on the bottom with a handwritten sentence:

You wanted to know.

THREE DAYS AFTER LUCAS walked away from me, I was still in defensive mode, hiding from any and all reality. I barely let Brayden in to check on me and he respected my space. He even held back on his feelings—how angry he was at Lucas—but I could see it in his eyes.

I'd been painting almost nonstop, because I didn't have to think to do that. Everything I did was dark and dreary, which wasn't a surprise. I'd never told Lucas to find the house in the commissioned picture and there were times over the past days where I nearly dropped it into a Google image search.

But a part of me didn't want to know. Not yet. Not now.

So when my phone rang and Gabrielle's number came up, I almost didn't answer it. She didn't know about me and Lucas, and I decided I wasn't ready to tell her.

But I picked up anyway, to see if she had any news about Jared. Gabrielle rushed in with, "Ryn, it's me. I only have a minute alone. I'm hiding in the bathroom—they'd kill me if they knew I was telling you this. Or anyone."

I knew exactly what she was about to tell me, but I still asked, "What's wrong? Are you okay?" because she might not be.

"I'm fine. I want to make sure you're okay." I wasn't sure how to answer that, but thankfully, she bulldozed past her question immediately. "Jared's missing."

I guessed that Jared's agent was done trying to keep his MIA status from the cast and crew and ultimately, the press. "He's still hiding out from you guys?" I asked tentatively.

"We thought that's what he was doing, but apparently he's actually missing."

My heart sank, because I'd been hoping that Jared was just hiding, out of embarrassment or even revenge against Lucas. "Missing? Are you sure?"

She lowered her voice even further. "The story was that he'd gone to his cabin to work on the script. He needed a couple of days, and we all figured we knew why. He checked in with his manager and his agent the night he left—the night of the fight with Lucas—but then he didn't show up for work today. He's not at his house either, and his computer and car are still at the cabin. His agent was pissed at him for missing an important talk show he'd been scheduled to do, and apparently she reported it to the police without anyone knowing, just in case."

"Just in case what?"

"I guess she thought that maybe Jared wasn't just in hiding."

My stomach tightened. "What are people saying?"

"That's why I'm calling you, Ryn. It's not good. The police were here earlier, before my call time. I heard Jared's agent mention the fight between Jared and Lucas. I heard they'd already sent someone to question Lucas."

I hated lying to her, but I didn't want to explain that they'd already spoken with Lucas. For all I knew, they were trying to find him again. Maybe that explained why I hadn't heard from him once since he'd walked out on me several days ago…or maybe that's what I wanted to believe, because I couldn't accept that he was giving up on us.

I didn't want to believe I could give up on us either.

After I hung up with Gabrielle, I took a long, hot shower to get rid of the kinks in my muscles and the fuzziness in my mind. I stayed under the spray for a long time, attempting to wash away all the bad feelings, but not wanting to leave the warmth.

Eventually, I did. Mainly because Brayden was bringing me dinner tonight, and he was coming into the apartment as I pulled my robe on and met him in the kitchen.

Grant was with him. I stared at both of them, confused. Brayden looked pale, and there was no takeout.

"What happened? What's wrong?" I demanded.

"I saw it on the monitor, Ryn, but I didn't see it happen," Brayden said. "We tried to rewind the tape but there's nothing there. One minute, nothing and the next..."

He pointed and my eyes followed.

On the carpet, another innocuous photo of the commissioned house.

Beyond that, a trail of daffodils along the hardwood floor.

The trail of my past led directly to my studio and filled me with fear and rage, a combination I wasn't sure what to do with.

You knew this could happen.

My body shook. I had a knife in my hands, certain I'd use it if called upon, despite the fact that both Brayden and Grant were here with me. I still stalked the apartment—my apartment—staking my claim.

It was only on my second round that I noticed there was blood on the flowers. Fresh blood.

Just like in your dreams.

"I think we need help," I heard Brayden say from behind me.

"Were you two together when you saw this?" I asked. The look that passed between Grant and Brayden was almost a dare. The tension threaded through me, but at least this soap opera was far more entertaining than the stalking crap.

Still, I didn't get my answer, not with Grant telling Brayden, "You need to tell her what you told me."

"Not yet," Brayden told him through gritted teeth.

Grant motioned in my direction and this Mexican standoff wasn't going anywhere without help. "Tell me what?"

Brayden cut his gaze in my direction and finally relented. "I've been getting letters at the gallery."

"Letters?"

He pressed his lips together in a grim line and my stomach plummeted. "That same photo of the house. And flower petals."

"What else?" I demanded.

He pulled a letter out of his pocket and handed it to me. I forced my fingers not to tremble (unsuccessfully) as I pulled out the heavily weighted vellum paper. Three words in clipped, striking penmanship.

There's no escape.

I don't remember much after that. I might've sunk to the floor or screamed or cursed or hit someone. But when I surfaced, I was lying, curled in a protective ball against the couch. My heart thudded heavily, but my body was numb.

Brayden had given me my pills. He'd had no choice. He'd called Dr. B and in the end, I'd agreed to the heavy darkness they'd bring me.

"Sleep, babe. We'll figure it out after you rest."

23

"LUCAS?"

"No sweetie, he's not here."

It took me a moment to surface from the heavy, numbing effect of the anxiety meds. It was like swimming in syrup, my eyelids dragging open slowly at the sound of Brayden's voice.

Brayden, not Lucas.

Brayden pressed his lips together in a small, concerned frown and handed me a ginger ale with a straw. I took a big sip.

It was tasteless and I was still floaty. "When will this shit wear off?"

"Soon. I only gave you half a pill. I had to."

"I know." I swallowed. "I can't stay here. I have to go."

Brayden didn't look surprised.

I went to the woods. Brayden didn't bother trying to talk me out of it—instead, he let Grant hire a driver to take me there and be at my disposal. The man's name was Deacon and he was a brick wall. Solid. Nothing would get through him, and Grant basically promised me as much.

Deacon checked my Catskills apartment before I went inside. He left me his number and a phone dedicated to him and then he went down the road to the inn. Because I'd told all of them I refused to work with a car sitting outside and watching me. My landlady was awesome—and an early-to-bed, early-to-rise, heavy sleeper, but I didn't want her to worry as to why I suddenly needed a bodyguard.

Of course, that didn't mean it wasn't happening.

After several hours of pacing and staring at the paintings I'd left here from last time, the thunder rolled outside. I tasted the electricity in the air that streamed in from the opened windows. The gauzy curtains filled with air, fluttering back and forth with the impending storm.

Danger was mounting, swirling around me. So was the frenzy and I was caught in its grasp, quite willingly. I gave myself over to it, sank into the creation and perversely let it sink its teeth into me and not let go. It would shake me around, leaving me beaten, bruised, exhausted…and oddly satiated. It wasn't unlike rough sex—amazing, intoxicatingly rough sex.

Hours later, covered in paint, the buzz in my brain returned, like a call that had been put on hold but now refused to wait any longer. Goose bumps covered my skin.

I felt watched.

He's here.

The feeling intensified as I walked outside, the damp morning air clinging to my skin. Everything was still fuzzy, including my head, but I wouldn't sleep for hours.

He's here, my mind persisted, unable to not listen to it. I kept painting.

He was closer than where the original man I'd seen all those years ago stood, close enough for me to know not to be frightened.

And yet, I was just as vulnerable now as I was then. I'd thought that would change over time.

It might've actually gotten worse.

He stood there, watching, waiting to be invited instead of simply barging in. I realized how long I'd been painting for, nearly nonstop since I'd arrived here…and that was well before sunrise. Now, I was seeing Lucas by the light of the moon.

"You're so beautiful," I murmured as he climbed up to the deck gracefully and closed the distance between us. In a flash, he'd lifted my T-shirt over my head, leaving me naked and raked by his gaze.

The rain, powerful and cleansing, began to pour down on our skin. Water droplets electrified and illuminated by lightning as the push-pull of nature against itself only intensified the feelings I had for Lucas.

I was still so angry with him. For hiding things from me. It still didn't make sense. What else were Lucas and Brayden hiding...about Bane? About each other?

But none of that mattered, because he was here. Protecting me, and letting me protect him.

Lucas held my hips, a crushing grip I savored, even as I knew I'd see his fingerprints on my hips in the morning. I wanted to. They were my badges of honor, my proof that Lucas Caine was mine. All mine.

Proof that I was all his.

I was up against the wall, helpless, legs spread, impaled on him as he drove into me with powerful, purposeful strokes.

When I came, it was with a yell, his name on my lips and it was *Lucas* and *yes* and *love you*. The look in his eyes, that pure masculine satisfaction, was unmistakable.

He came with a groan, a roar of need that echoed in the woods that surrounded us.

He's here.

When the sex ended, reality began to sift back in, slowly. Still, what would've been an angry demand tapered to immediate concern as I asked, "What are you doing here? What's wrong?"

He looked tired. Haunted. There was a bruise on his cheek and I didn't know why. "You weren't at your apartment," was all he said.

"I didn't expect you back." There was no recrimination in my tone but he finished my thought for me.

"Because I never let you know when that'll be."

"Yeah, but that's okay. I didn't leave to scare you."

"You came here to paint."

"Yes."

"I won't bother you."

But I was tugging him inside. He didn't put up much of a fight. The rain ultimately pushed us inside. Soaked, we stood together for several minutes and I knew I needed to do whatever it took to wipe that haunted, hunted look from his eyes.

Later, I would learn that Lucas was far from hunted, and that this was a situation when I could discover what happened when a hunter got captured by his prey.

For now, we had things to discuss, things that could come between us, rip us apart, but I refused to harp on.

All the hours I'd spent alone here, wondering who was out there watching me—from the beginning, Lucas had felt like that man. Now, I wasn't sure I wanted to know if he was…because he'd become that man for me. That's all that mattered. "Where have you been?"

"Work," he said distractedly. "Things to take care of."

"You look tired."

"Just a rough couple of days. Haven't been sleeping much." He rubbed his eyes.

"Do you want to sleep now?"

"Not sure I can."

"Come on." I brought him into the bathroom with the big, old-fashioned claw-footed tub and ran the water. He stood obediently—not like him at all—until I helped him undress. He shrugged off the layers and climbed into the tub, rested his head back and groaned.

A good groan. A contented one. I'd caused them enough to know.

Gently, I began to massage his feet, using the body wash he used. I'd brought it with me, telling myself that was because I didn't have soap here. But that was a lie. I wanted to bring a piece of him here with me.

I moved to his shoulders. He leaned forward, catching his arms around his knees, letting me knead the sore, tense muscles. The knots disappeared under my fingertips.

"You're wasting your hands on me," he protested, but he didn't make a move to stop me.

"Comforting you's never a waste." I soaped up his hair, washed it, poured water from a pitcher to rinse it.

"One day, you might feel differently," he murmured. His words made me cold, but when his eyes opened and his gaze met mine, it was so full of fire I could burn in it.

"Never," I told him fiercely. "Never."

24

DRAINED, WE LAY TOGETHER on the soft braided rug. Lucas pulled the comforter over us and we remained skin to skin as the rain drove against the windowsills as if it wanted in so desperately.

But we were protected from the elements, or so I believed at that point. I'd started to drift off when the knocking woke me. I tried ignoring it, but it was loud and persistent, and I opened my eyes to see if Lucas was hearing it.

But I was alone. The bathroom door was closed, a sliver of light peeking out from under it. The shower was running. Sighing, I wrapped the comforter around myself and jerked the door open, sure it was either Susan or the landlady, both of whom were known to bring me food at odd hours.

But it wasn't either woman. It was Dan Turner. I went to slam the door, but he was fast, his meaty palm preventing me from doing so.

"Jared Connor is dead," he said bluntly.

I took a step back—stumbled, really, as the breath rushed from my lungs as though it'd been forcibly squeezed out. "What...how?" I finally managed.

"He was murdered."

"Murdered," I repeated.

"Lucas Caine is a primary suspect." When Turner mentioned Lucas's name, I instinctively glanced toward the bathroom door. Before I could protest, Turner was walking through my place, slamming his fist against the bathroom door, gun drawn.

Gun *drawn*.

"What are you doing? Why do you have a gun?" I demanded, but he was ignoring me in favor of opening the door.

"Because your boyfriend's a dangerous man," Turner finally told me as he stared into the empty bathroom. Lucas was gone. I didn't have time to ponder why before it was Turner's turn to do some demanding of me. "Where is he?"

"I don't know." I pulled the comforter tighter. "You're not the police. You can't come in here with a gun and arrest him."

His expression tightened menacingly. "Little girl, you have no idea what I can do. You'd better get your story straight or you'll be sitting in a cell next to him."

My back went up. "I'll call the police right now to discuss it. He was with me all night."

I regretted the words as soon as they left my mouth.

"You're alibiing Lucas Caine." Turner smiled, but it didn't reach his eyes. "I'd be careful, Ryn. If he comes back, call the police."

But Lucas wouldn't—I knew he'd never put me in danger like that.

It didn't mean I wouldn't be there for him. "It's a far cry from fistfight to murder," I told Turner as he walked out the door.

He looked over his shoulder as he kept walking. "Not if he's been convicted of murder previously."

I shut the door so Turner wouldn't see me sink to my knees, the bile rising in my throat as his words echoed in my head.

**Turn the page for a sneak peek of
Book 2 in the trilogy, PIECES OF ME,
coming Fall 2016 from Stephanie Tyler.**

pieces of *Me*

A **SHELTER** NOVEL

We could destroy each other...

Lucas Caine is the most complicated, intense man I'd ever known...and the only one capable of freeing me from my past.

We had more in common than I could know. Both damaged by our childhoods, we put up shields to keep the world away. But I was defenseless against him.

What I didn't know was that he was equally so against me.

Prologue

14 years earlier

Bane was already outside Lucas's house when he'd run out of it and vomited in the bushes. He'd still been on his knees when he noticed Bane's old jalopy of a car idling in the street like a fucking angel's wing.

Lucas didn't hesitate. He had the clothes on his back, the bag he'd grabbed on the way out and some money. He hadn't taken all of it, instead shoved it into the littler kids' pockets for them to have when they woke.

He'd made Bane stop several blocks away so he could call the police too, because someone needed to be there for those kids.

He'd left the front door open so no one would scare them and he'd detailed to the police what he'd seen in the house, emphasizing that there were little kids inside who were sleeping. Who'd be scared—"scarred for life"—if the police came blazing in.

As he got back into Bane's car, he could only hope for the best. For both of them. Bane was holding his arm at an unnatural angle and they both ignored that and the slate of bruises turning colors on the side of his face.

Instead, Lucas stared at the blood on his own hands as they drove through the night.

ALSO BY STEPHANIE TYLER:

DON'T MISS **MIRROR ME**:
BOOK 1 IN THE MIRROR SERIES,
ON SALE NOW

Kayla Peters hasn't been Claire Cooper for six years…but the past is about to catch up with her, and nothing will ever be the same.

Kayla's in witness protection, being hidden from her twin sister by the US Marshals Office. When Kayla moves in next to a former Special Forces operative, she discovers that he's got a dark, dangerous past of his own…and that he might be the only person who can help her survive.

Teige doesn't want to like Kayla. Since the death of his CO and Teige's retirement from Delta Force, he's been taking on the most dangerous jobs, pressing the luck he feels has followed him his entire life. He's convinced it'll run out, because he knows no one can be that lucky all the time. And when he discovers who Kayla really is, and what kind of trouble's following her, he realizes he's up against the most dangerous—and personal—job of his career.

ALSO BY
STEPHANIE TYLER:

Shelter Series
SHELTER ME
PIECES OF ME (coming Fall 2016)

Mirror Series
MIRROR ME
RULE OF THIRDS
WALK IN MY SHADOW *(coming September 2016)*

Skulls Creek MC Series
VIPERS RUN
VIPERS RULE

Section 8 Series
SURRENDER
UNBREAKABLE
FRAGMENTED

Defiance Series
DEFIANCE
REDEMPTION
SALVATION
TEMPERANCE

Dire Wolves Series
DIRE WARNING (prequel novella)
DIRE NEEDS
DIRE WANTS
DIRE DESIRES

Shadow Force Series
LIE WITH ME
PROMISES IN THE DARK
IN THE AIR TONIGHT
NIGHT MOVES
LONELY IS THE NIGHT

Hold Series
HARD TO HOLD
TOO HOT TO HOLD
HOLD ON TIGHT
HOLDING ON (novella)

Hot Nights, Dark Desires Anthology
NIGHT VISION (novella)

Harlequin Blaze
COMING UNDONE
RISKING IT ALL
BEYOND HIS CONTROL

WRITING AS SE JAKES

Men of Honor Series
BOUND BY HONOR
BOUND BY LAW
TIES THAT BIND
BOUND BY DANGER
BOUND FOR KEEPS
BOUND TO BREAK

Phoenix, Inc. Series
NO BOUNDARIES

WRITING AS
SYDNEY CROFT

TEMPTING THE FIRE
TAKEN BY FIRE
THREE THE HARD WAy (novella)

Hot Nights, Dark Desires Anthology
SHADOW PLAY (novella)

ABOUT THE AUTHOR

STEPHANIE TYLER is the *New York Times* bestselling author of romance novels spanning multiple genres, including Romantic Suspense, New Adult, Paranormal Romance and Contemporary Romance. She's a hybrid author who writes for multiple publishers, including Random House, NAL/Penguin, Harlequin, Carina Press, Mammoth Books, Belle Books and Samhain Publishing, as well as Riptide (as SE Jakes) and indie publishing. Her books have been translated into half a dozen languages, nominated for an RT Readers' Choice Award and garnered top picks from *RT Book Magazine* as well as starred reviews from *Publishers Weekly*. She's a frequent workshop presenter and has contributed stories for anthologies for charities, including **SEAL of My Dreams**, which has raised over 150K for the Veterans Medical Association.

SE JAKES is the pen name for *New York Times* bestselling author Stephanie Tyler, and half the co-writing team of Sydney Croft. First published in 2011, SE Jakes has quickly risen to be a bestselling author in the LGBT romance genre, as well as a fan favorite. Her books are frequently highlighted in *USA Today* and have been reviewed by *Library Journal* and *RT Books Magazine*. She's been nominated by several sites for Favorite M/M author and has finaled in the Goodreads M/M Romance Readers Choice Awards in 7 categories. She's a hybrid author who writes for Riptide Publishing and Samhain Publishing, and she indie publishes as well.

SYDNEY CROFT is the alter ego of Stephanie Tyler and Larissa Ione, two *New York Times* bestselling authors who blend their very different writing interests into adventurous tales of erotic paranormal fiction. Together, they developed a world where people with extraordinary abilities, like the power to control storms, could live and work with others like them. The series has been described as "Erotica meets the X-Men," and is unique in its own "erotic superhero romance" niche. Larissa and Stephanie live in different states and communicate almost entirely through email, though they often get together for conferences and book signings.